WILLIAM EDMONDS

# THE WIZARD AND THE BEAR

iUniverse, Inc.
New York   Bloomington

iUniverse books may be ordered through booksellers or by contacting:

iUniverse
1663 Liberty Drive
Bloomington, IN 47403
www.iuniverse.com
1-800-Authors (1-800-288-4677)

Because of the dynamic nature of the Internet, any Web addresses or links contained in this book may have changed since publication and may no longer be valid. The views expressed in this work are solely those of the author and do not necessarily reflect the views of the publisher, and the publisher hereby disclaims any responsibility for them.

ISBN: 978-1-4502-6924-7 (sc)
ISBN: 978-1-4502-6925-4 (hc)
ISBN: 978-1-4502-6926-1 (ebook)

Printed in the United States of America

iUniverse rev. date: 12/07/2010

Dedication: To Julie, who urged me to be a writer.

# Chapter 1

## *The Ghost Singer*

A wailing cry came on the prairie breeze and Gray Bear awoke, his skin crawling with fear. He had dozed off to the howling of coyotes, the cries of night hawks and the monotonous chanting of whip-poor-wills, but now the creatures of the summer night were quiet, as if they had stilled their voices to listen. The wind rose and the rustling of the sumac leaves above his grassy bed masked the mystery sound. But soon the wind died and the cries came again, shrill, rising and falling with a drum-beat rhythm. Gray Bear lay there on his back with his heart thumping hard. He stared up fixedly at the starry sky as if he were afraid to look to right or left. The wind rose again and hid the mysterious sound. He snatched the edge of the deerskin blanket away from his face and reached for a weapon. In the instant of awakening he had been a frightened boy, but as his strong right hand gripped the handle of his hatchet he remembered he was old enough to be a warrior. But the fear remained. It was the kind of fear even warriors can admit to: ghost fear, fear of spirits prowling in the night. And as the coyotes began to howl again they lifted their voices together in a clamor like the barking of village dogs when strangers are approaching. He muttered to himself, "This is a bad place. Spirits are warning me to leave."

A forest loomed nearby. He felt a natural urge to hide himself among the trees. He rose to his knees and gathered his equipment, a sturdy bow of the yellow wood of boise d'arc, a panther-skin quiver of turkey-feathered arrows, and a light sleeping blanket of doe skin. He draped the blanket around his shoulders and felt of the decorative tuft on top of his head to make sure it was standing properly upright, a warning to any enemy that he was armed and dangerous. Then he crept away through the tall prairie grass, going, un-thinking, like a hunted animal, toward the nearby woods. The forest was a place of darkness and unknown perils but also a hiding place away from the prairie that seemed as bright as day under the rising moon. Inside the grove he walked among tree trunks that towered up blacker than the surrounding darkness. High overhead the wind surged through the treetops with a rushing, sighing sound. Moonbeams found their way down through the swaying boughs and splashed wildly-moving patterns of light on the forest floor.

Between the gusts of wind he could still hear the mysterious voice. It was a ghost, he thought. No living person would be singing here in the night, far from any lodge or village. The wind died completely for a while and the mystery sound came clearly to his ears. It was a mournful chant. The high notes rose like the howls of a wolf. The low notes growled like an angry bear. He stood, open mouthed, listening. Again, the skin of his back and neck crawled with fear. "I know that voice," he muttered, "That is Old Monkon singing! He is chanting a medicine song. But Old Monkon is dead!" In his imagination he saw again the wise old shaman lying in the door of the medicine lodge. His sobbing wife told how her man had tried to fight the hateful raiders and how those ugly warriors had laughed as they were killing the weak old man.

Gray Bear muttered to himself: "What is that ghost trying to tell me? Shall I go back? Shall I give up this mission? Shall I go on, hoping a friendly spirit is protecting me? Ah-ee, I don't know what to do. I must ask someone older and wiser about this thing. I will go back and ask my father."

Alone there in the dark he felt his face grow hot with shame. If he turned back now, only a day's journey from home, everyone would think he was a coward. In his imagination he seemed to hear his father's voice, saying, "My son, the spirit watchers see everything you do. Always they look for signs of fear or weakness. If you turn back because you are afraid, if you run away when you should stand and fight, they will remember. And when you stand before your brothers and boast of what you have done, those spirits will change the shape of your tongue and everyone who hears your voice will know that you are lying."

Gray Bear turned toward the place from which the chanting came. He lifted his face as if to speak to the treetops or the sky. He growled in a fierce, unnatural voice, the voice assumed by the bear men in their mystery rituals, "See me, watchers, and see that I am not afraid! I was named for an old bear, wise with age, a bear that prowls at night, fearing nothing. Look at me! See I have no fear" He started forward trough the darkness under the trees, going directly toward the ghostly sound. His legs felt stiff as though they did not want to walk. His feet stumbled over vines and fallen branches. He felt a sudden anger at his own legs and feet. It was as though they belonged to someone who was afraid. Instinctively, he stooped low as he walked, though he knew it was futile to hide from a spirit. He had pulled his blanket so high it had become a hood covering his head. He was perspiring but his teeth chattered with a nervous chill. Now he was approaching an opening in the forest, a place where a powerful storm of some past season had broken big trees and thrown them to the ground. They were lying now like a pile of huge sticks, their dead trunks and their upward-reaching limbs covered with leafy vines. The dismal chanting seemed to be coming from just across the clearing. He stooped, lower and lower, as he crept around the edge of the fallen trees. If there had been eyes to see him he would have looked, not like a man, but like some strange, humped beast creeping through the darkness. Suddenly he became aware that a dark shape was moving on the ground as if some man-sized figure were flattening itself and sliding into deeper shadows under a tree. As he stared at the apparition he was astonished to see that it was thrusting toward him two big arms holding out a bow, a drawn bow, parallel to the ground. Back of the bow the thing was formless, headless, the darkest shadow under the low hung boughs of the trees. And it was pointing an arrow straight at him!

Gray Bear's mouth gaped open as he tried to yell, but his throat seemed to be squeezed shut. Only a moan came from his lips. He stood, as still as a stump, his eyes straining to open wider. Then he saw the moonlight flash on a glassy arrow point and his warrior's training moved him. He dodged to one side, twisting his body to present a narrower target. With the action he found his voice; he shrilled the wild, instinctive cry that a man might use to bluff an attacking animal. Even as he turned and yelled he saw the bow snap straight and the arrow was there beside him, buzzing like a giant insect, stinging his side near to his heart.

After that he heard his own voice mourning, "A demon has killed me!" But he was the son and grandson of fierce warriors, so with his face contorted, his lips drawn back, he howled the battle cry of his people and, swinging his war axe high above his head, he charged like a pain-crazed beast at the thing that had shot him.

# Chapter 2

## *The Dreamer*

His name, in a language of the northern plains, meant "thunder rumbling softly in the distance which does not come any closer." He was sick and starving and far from home. In the heat of afternoons he crouched on a dog skin robe just outside the entrance of the cave. It was pleasant to sit there in the shade of an oak tree, with sunlight through the leaves casting a flickering pattern on the ground. Sometimes he dozed and dreamed. Sometimes he seemed to be dreaming when he was awake. Big dogs were lying about the campsite. They had dug shallow pits beneath the bushes in which they lay with their bodies pressed against the coolness of the freshly exposed earth. They were like wolves now, going forth from time to time to hunt in their small pack. They were well-fed. The man envied them.

In his loneliness he had grown fond of the dogs. When he wandered near them in the campsite they would raise their heads, roll their eyes to show rims of white, and thump the ground with their tails. He would greet each of them by name and pause to make a few idle remarks.

"Hee, Yellow Face, I see you are the chief. I see the others follow when you go to hunt. Ha, Black Dog, you are getting fat! You should bring some meat back to me. I am one who needs it. I see you, Scarred Back! You look more like a wolf now than a travois dog. Soon I will harness you again to the dragging poles. We must march away, up this river, before the first moon of the cold time rises in the sky."

In the cool of morning, while the dogs were hunting, he foraged in the nearby woods, seeking the edible fungus that grows on logs, odorous lily roots, and the few berries which were ripe in this season. He ate the fat grubs which turned up with his digging and the long-legged locusts when he could catch them. But he was too weak to forage as a strong person would have done. He could collect barely enough food to keep himself alive, not enough to build his strength. From time to time he thought about killing one of the dogs for food. But they were stronger than he and they had become his only companions. In the afternoons he did not feel like moving so he rested and thought and dreamed and, more and more, developed the peculiar habit of talking to imaginary companions. Sometimes he would sit there staring into the empty space before his eyes, seeing listeners to whom he told long stories. Often he repeated the story of how he had come to be here in this place, alone in a land of enemies, weak and starving in the midst of plenteous summer. Now he was starting on this story once again.

"Ho, listen to me. I have much to tell about a journey to a distant land. Ayee, that was a strange land, far away, where big trees grow as many as the blades of grass here in our homeland. Yes, hear me and you will learn of things you have never seen and will never see. This is the way it happened: When the planting moon was in the sky, the chiefs chose me to go far off toward the lands where the sun goes in winter. They wanted to know when the buffalo would come and if our enemies along the White Flat River were planting corn or were preparing for war. Those chiefs chose me because they trusted me; they knew my eyes are good, that I am strong, that I would not turn back and run in fear at the first sign of enemies. I tell you they chose well!

I went far south along the Creek of Aspens. Waded the Big White River and still marched on. At last I saw a town with big lodges made of earth. I knew it was a place where Pawnee's lived, but I was not afraid. I saw some people working, planting corn. I crept up close and watched them. I was so close I could hear them talking. But of course I could not understand their speech. I hid in bushes until the sun went down. I claim a coup for this! Who else has gone into the Pawnee fields and listened to them talk?

I started back to tell the chiefs that the buffalo were many and our enemies were growing corn. But on my homeward journey I came upon some people traveling south. They were paddling canoes along the Creek of Aspens. I saw them first and watched them and they did not know that I was there. They were strange to see, those people, three or four men and one big dog in each canoe. I knew that they were northern men, the people who always want their dogs nearby to guard their camp at night and to pull travois, or sledges, if they lose canoes. These men were of the small Elk River Tribe. They are the ones who always offer to help us when we go to war. Ha, they are wise to do this for they need strong friends. They need brave friends to fight their enemies!

I hailed them and they greeted me with grins and friendly gestures. They urged me to come with them to their night camp. They offered food and said we could sit and talk beside the fire. I saw that they were youngsters who had not yet won their warriors symbols. They saw that I was a warrior and treated me with great respect.

That night they told me they were going far away to the down-river country that is beyond the Pawnee lands, even beyond the place where the Flat White River runs into The Big Muddy River. They had heard that the people on that big river make the finest canoes in all of the world. It was their plan to capture some of those canoes and bring them home filled with trophies, with weapons and maybe even prisoners. They said they had to go far off to win their warrior's honors because their chiefs had forbidden them to stir up trouble with nearby tribes. They said that when they did this thing they would be rewarded with the symbols of manhood; that all the people would talk about them and that the maidens who were old enough for marriage would look at them with admiration. They laughed when they said this last thing the way warriors always make light of their interest in women, it being of no importance since marriages are arranged for them by their fathers and uncles.

They listened to me while I told them of how my own father had gone, long ago, drifting down the rivers in his canoe. Truly, he went so far it took him a whole summer to return. I told them many things my father had told me about that distant land on the Great Smoky River.

When they heard these things, they begged me to go with them to guide them. They reminded me of the many times their warriors have come to help my people with our wars. They said if I would go with them I would be their leader.

Before we slept, I promised to go with them far enough to show them how to pass the Pawnee towns. But I said I would have to turn back then because the chiefs of my people were waiting to hear the news that I would bring.

They said, "That is good. You are our leader. It will be as you say." But when we came to the valley of the Flat White River, we found that it was flooded. Water covered all the lands beside the river as far as we could see. They paddled out into that water for a great distance and came to a place where it was rushing along, brown with mud, carrying dead buffalo and whole trees. Ho, those foolish young men paddled their canoes right into the swift-flowing water. They paddled as hard as they could, rushing along faster then the moving water, going toward the east. They laughed and shouted like crazy men and raced with one another. Hee! They wanted to be recognized as men and warriors but they were acting like children playing in a place of great danger. I could have ordered them to stop their foolish behavior. They had said I was their leader but then they would have thought I was afraid. I kept silent and showed them that I was not afraid of fast water.

We traveled far that day. When the sun went down we were in an unfamiliar land. There were big trees everywhere. The brown water of the river covered the land under the trees. There was an evil smell all about and I knew this was a place of bad medicine. But I was not afraid. We found a hill rising from the water and camped there. We built a fire and the young men laughed and bragged about how brave they had been to travel in that swift water. When I told them I must now go back to my own people, they began to laugh. They pointed at the flood waters all around and asked me how far I could swim.

I was very angry. Their leader was frightened by my anger and became respectful again. He said, "Surely you see we cannot send one canoe back now. We need every man to help with this mission. We have come far today. The place where we are going cannot be far from here. Stay with us! You are our chief! Lead us on this raid, than we will all go back together. All of us want to follow you!"

I was still very angry. They said I was their chief. It seemed to me I was their prisoner. But I knew that even if I took a canoe from them by force, I could not use it to go home while the river was flooding. So I said, "I will stay with you until the flood is over. If we find a town to raid I will lead you. After that you will take me home very fast or I will go back to my people and tell them you made me a prisoner and brought me to this place. If I do that there will be war between our peoples! Oh, I was still very angry!"

The starving man grew tired of talking to his imaginary listeners. His voice had grown faint. Now he became quiet, his eyes closed, his head sagged forward and he slept. Birds called in the treetops, the cicadas buzzed and the wind whispered in the quivering cottonwood leaves.

His story must have continued in his dreams for after a while he awakened, jerking his head upright and calling out, "Ho, that was a fight! Those Smoky River People came after us like wolves following an injured elk. They came to punish us for raiding their village. Their warriors returned, from wherever they were, to find their women and children crying, their lodges burning. Ho, they were very angry. They followed us for days. Then one morning, as the sun was rising, they came rushing out of the trees around out camp. They came, swinging big war clubs and screaming like panthers.

I stood and faced them. I shouted to my companions to stand and fight. Ha, those Elk River boys ran like rabbits. They yelled at one another and ran to their canoes. Two enemy men rushed at me, the rest chased the young men down to the water. I could hear a fight there on the river's edge but I could not turn to look. I was fighting two men who were trying to kill me. I backed slowly toward the river, then into the water. I was bleeding and bruised but I did not turn my back on those enemies. I did not flee. No, the water became too deep for standing and I fell, sank under the water, than swam away. There was an empty canoe there drifting in the river. I clung to it, I could not climb in, and paddled with my hands and kicked it into the main current of the river. I saw the last of the Elk River boys. They were paddling upstream in four canoes. They had left their wounded, their dogs, and me. They were paddling very hard. The dogs were swimming in the water too. They had tried to follow the canoes upstream, now they turned with the current and followed me. I swam across to the other side of that big river and then got into the canoe. I had no paddle, so all day I floated down the stream, staying on the opposite side from my enemies. The river was taking me back toward their village but I could not paddle. I was injured too badly to go on shore and walk. I floated half the night, than crawled ashore to die. But I found a cave where I could hide and the dogs, which had followed me along the bank of the river, came into the cave with me. I lay down with them to keep warm. One of those dogs was badly hurt. Soon it died. This is its skin I am sitting on now. This is the cave!"

The man suddenly looked surprised at his own words. He was bewildered. How could he be talking to the people in his own village if he was here by the cave far from home? He looked around searchingly to confirm where he was. Then he looked at the sun and saw it was low in the sky. He felt a chill, either real or imaginary, and said, "I must build a fire."

He liked to build a small fire each evening. It was a foolish thing to do here in the land of his enemies but his mind was not working well. In his confusion and loneliness he thought it would be a good thing to see people, any people, again. But he kept the fire small and always quenched it carefully before he went into the cave to sleep.

When the fire had burned for only a short time the dogs began to bark. In his imagination he seemed to see people approaching the cave. He was terrified. He had a bow and a few arrows which he had retrieved from the canoe before he sent it floating down the river. He might still be too weak to draw the bow, but his warrior's training was guiding his actions now. Clutching the bow and a few arrows he hurried into the woods to hide.

# Chapter 3

## *The Wizard*

Gray Bear raced forward, yelling like a warrior in a battle charge. His terror had been transformed into a crazed desire to strike the enemy. The blackberry tangle blocked his way and he leaped, knees and arms flung high, warclub brandished overhead. For an instant he was like a furious eagle, soaring and screaming. His yell ended in a grunt as the club was torn from his hand by solid impact with a low-hung bough. He was tipped backward by the shock and fell on his back among the thorns. Though momentarily helpless, he still tried to fight. He kicked violently at the shadows around him, drew and stabbed with his skinning knife. He threw himself forward and rose into a crouch, then froze in that position, motionless, glaring into the menacing darkness His enemy had vanished. Around him the woods were silent, except for the chirping of the small insects that have no interest in the affairs of men. No doubt the larger creatures, those with fur or feathers, were cringing in fright at his loud yells. There was only a faint sound of the wind soughing in the leaves high overhead and from far away came the cries of coyotes, still praying to the moon. Now in the aftermath of terror, rage and injury Gray Bear was sick. He was actually trembling with an unfamiliar weakness and his stomach was threatening to empty itself of whatever he had eaten before going to sleep. For him, such feelings of malaise were almost unknown. He was frightened that the demon might have put some evil spell on him. Like an injured animal he sought a hiding place, creeping into the deepest shadows under the low hung boughs of a huge maple. He crouched, perfectly still, pressing the soft leather of his sleeping blanket against the wound in his side, murmuring prayers inside his head to the only comforting thing he had seen in this night of terror, the serene face of Grandmother Moon. Soon the forest creatures began to stir again. A fearless skunk came lumbering into a pool of moonlight, rolling small logs and pouncing on the fleeing beetles. It flaunted the banner of its white-stripped tail, a warning to bobcats and foxes of the terrible punishment it could deal to any attacker. A fox, as silent as a shadow, came trotting across the glade. It stopped and stared suspiciously at the dark place where Gray Bear was hiding Time passed; the tranquil moon moved to the west and looked down through another opening in the boughs. Nearby a Barred Owl called three quick bursts of hoots, like guffaws of ghostly laughter in the darkness.

Gray Bear's head snapped up. A barred owl usually gives four quick hoots, pauses, than repeats its call. The people say they always count to eight. But warriors or hunters in the same dank river forests call to one another with hoots of unusual number. Three sets of hoots usually means "I am here, where are you?" Gray Bear responded, mimicking the wild call perfectly. There was an immediate response, an imitation of the sound Gray Bear had made. He muttered, "That was not an owl," and stared intently in the direction of the call. Soon a dark figure came walking through the shadows directly toward his hiding place. Gray Bear stared in wonder; this person was walking through the dark woods as casually as one would stroll along a village path. The unknown was a person of small stature with no decorations on his head. For a moment Gray Bear thought it was a woman, then bright moonlight lit the face and his wonder turned to disgust and anger. It was his own half brother, the would-be magician and medicine man, a trickster and troublemaker, the one called Little Owl.

"Why are you here?" hissed Gray Bear. He spoke in a whisper because he still felt some evil thing was nearby but his anger almost overcame his fear. "You have been following me! You know our father sent me along on this mission. He said it was a thing one warrior could do. You have followed me before and made trouble for me. I will stand for no more of your tricks!"

The small man pretended to be surprised. "Are you a warrior now? I didn't know you had won your feather. And I do not see it now. Have you lost it?" He continued in a more serious vein. "I came here to confer with the spirits of the caves. As you know they leave the caves when Grandfather Sun has disappeared. I watched them leave this night. They are everywhere in the forest now, flying around in the darkness, looking for foolish people. But they know me; I don't need to fear them. While I was listening to their voices I heard loud screams of fear coming from the woods by the river. Some man or boy was yelling in terror. And in the midst of the loud screams I heard a familiar war cry. I waited a while, hoping the bat sprits would tell me what had happened. When they said it was safe for me to do so, I gave the rallying call of the Barred Owl. I heard your answer and came here to find you."

Gray Bear said, angrily, "I did not yell in fear! All warriors yell when they are fighting an enemy. You know nothing about these things because you can never be a warrior."

Little Owl responded calmly. "I know about these things. But I do not want to be a warrior. I am important to warriors. They need me to treat their wounds. The Great Spirit made my right arm weak so I cannot draw a bow. He did this so I would be a medicine man. Ah ee! He saved me from all the pain that warriors must suffer. This is good. I am glad!"

Gray Bear responded, "You have not treated any warrior's wounds. You are only a boy!"

"I am older than you." snapped Little Owl, "I was born in the moon of short days, you in the planting moon. The people still remember how proud our father was that both his wives had given him sons in the same year."

Gray Bear thought of something very ugly to say, about his fathers sorrow that one of his sons could never be a warrior, but he decided it would be better to keep still.

Little Owl continued, "Tell me why you were doing all that yelling. What did you see?" Gray Bear was still feeling angry but he discovered he wanted to talk about his terrible experience.

He said, "There was a spirit thing, I don't know what to call it, it was low down on the ground like a crouching beast. It had three arms, maybe more. I saw two hands holding a bow and another one must have been drawing the arrow. It had no head that I could see but there was an eye, I think. I saw something like a big eye gleaming."

"Well, you had better forget about what you have seen," said Little Owl, "It might be very bad for you to talk about this thing. You might make the spirit very angry. Then he will come some night and drain out all of your blood."

Gray Bear exclaimed, "Ho! That is what the spirit tried to do tonight! See the wound here in my side. It is still bleeding." Little Owl came forward at once with an air of professional interest. He shoved Gray Bear roughly out into the moonlight. He began to poke with his fingers at the place where the arrow had done its damage. He muttered magic words that Gray Bear could not understand. After causing much discomfort, he finally said, "Hee, this is nothing. The arrow grazed your ribs. A warrior must get many wounds worse than this one before he is old. Ay-ee, I am glad I am not a warrior!" He took some sticky ointment from one of the leather bags he was carrying on his belt and smeared it on the wound. To Gray Bear's surprise, the pain stopped almost at once. Gray Bear was grateful for this and looked at his half-brother with a new respect. He decided he could use further magic. He said, "my warclub is gone, It flew off into the darkness while I was fighting. Can you use your magic powers to find it for me?"

Little Owl frowned and said, "Even warriors of importance are not helped by the spirits when they are careless and lose their weapons. You will have to wait until Grandfather Sun returns, then go and find it yourself. I cannot help you. The spirits laugh at warriors - at fighters who are clumsy."

Gray Bear's anger flared again. If one of his peers, a would-be warrior, had called him clumsy, there would have been a fight. But he did not know how to cope with this soft-looking non-warrior with the sharp tongue. Certainly there was no honor to be gained by striking him. Instead he drew himself up like a chief about to make an important announcement. He said, "I am going now. You, Little Owl, can stay here and talk with the bats. It will do you no good to try to follow me. I know how to hide my tracks so no man can follow. Now I am going. That is all I have to say."

Little Owl responded at once and his voice was firm. He too sounded like a chief giving commands. He said, "Do not call me Little Owl! Call me Monkon. And know that I was sent here by the spirits to help you. Listen! It is a good thing you are going on this mission. But the spirits have told me it will be much more difficult than you thought. They have told me you need a medicine man to help you or you will surely fail. Now think how I have already helped you. Did I not treat your wound? Did I not stop the pain and the bleeding? Now there is more I must do for you. You must eat so you will be strong again. See here, I have trail food made by the wife of Crow Who Talks. This is a food made for the strongest warriors. It is so strong you can eat only a little or it will make you sick. Yes, you must eat and drink before you sleep. There is a brook in that gully that runs down to the river. The water is clean. Now you will eat and drink, then you will sleep. When you awaken you will be strong again!"

Gray Bear wanted to refuse the food but it was strange how he reached out for it as though his hand were taking orders from his stomach. He felt a curious lassitude, as though he could not resist his brother's commands. He chewed the strong, dark food then drank some water and almost at once he felt his eyelids trying to close. It seemed to him that he had never been so sleepy.

Little Owl led the way to a hidden place under a tangle of grapevines. Gray Bear rolled himself in his blanket and went to sleep at once. The medicine man lay beside him but he did not sleep for a long time. He lay there listening to, and arguing with, the spirit voices in his mind.

# Chapter 4

## *The Stranger*

When the first light of dawn came to the woods, Gray Bear was already awake. He was crouched under a cottonwood tree sniffing the morning breeze and listening intently for unusual sounds. His brother had said strangers were camped nearby and he was determined to see them before they had a chance to see him. As the light grew the woods became quite noisy. Crows called raucously and a gray squirrel was chattering with sharp bird-like notes. A redbird was caroling in a tree over the place where he had expected to hear evidence of the nearby strangers. Little Owl was still sleeping soundly. He was wrapped in his deer skin robe and, to Gray Bear's disgust, he was snoring softly. Finally, Gray Bear reached over with his bow and rapped his brother on the sole of an exposed foot. This was a bad move, as Little Owl yelped with pain. Gray Bear hissed at him to be still, after which both bothers crouched silently for a while, listening for some reaction to the yelp. There was none. So Little Owl arose and produced a pouch of parched corn for their breakfast. He seemed to be carrying a treasure trove of food and medicine in various pouches that were attached to his belt.

After they had eaten and had a drink of water from the nearby stream, Gray Bear was ready for action. He commanded Little Owl to stay where he was, then moved off through the forest, seeking a place directly down wind from the stranger's camp. He stopped when his nose detected the odor of charred wood and ashes, evidence that a camp fire had been burning recently, perhaps the evening before, but not now.

Gray Bear turned to his brother, who had been following him, and spoke. He was so intent on the business at hand that he seemed not to notice that Little Owl had ignored the command to remain where he was. He said, "Ho! No one is there. No morning fire. No people. No dogs. Those people have gone away."

Little Owl responded, sulkily, "Ha! This is not so. They are still there. They built no morning fire because they heard your screams of terror in the night. You frightened those people when you screamed like a woman attacked by a bear."

Gray Bear flushed red with anger. He glared a t his brother as if he would like to strike him but he said nothing for a while. When he finally spoke he assumed the manner of a chief addressing his men. "What would I do if I were a chief there in that camp, ah? In the night I heard fierce war cries in the woods nearby. A brave warrior with a strong voice is fighting something there. I wait; I listen until the night is finished. Then I lead my men into the woods. Before I go I tell the women not to start the morning fires. Now I go, looking for that warrior with a strong voice. I go toward the direction from which the war cries came."

Little Owl interrupted. He was looking contemptuous. He said, "No one left that camp. Dogs are still guarding it. I am saying what I know."

Gray Bear said, "I will go and see about this thing. You stay here. I do not want your clumsy footsteps making a noise behind me." He turned and faced directly into the wind He knew how hard it would be to spy on a camp guarded by dogs but he was confident of his skill as a stalker. He moved forward, placing each foot on the ground, toes first, with great care. Half stooping, he turned his shoulders from side to side to avoid moving the low hanging branches. He kept the wind full in his face so that it whispered equally in both his ears.

But that wind was making a mockery of his caution. It was going directly from him to the place down wind where the dogs had gone at sunrise to hunt for game, an opossum perhaps or a rabbit for their breakfast. Now those dogs stopped suddenly and stood, with their heads lifted, sniffing the breeze. The hair on their backs rose and growls rumbled in their throats. Then they came charging through the trees leaping over low bushes. They made fierce huffing sounds with the effort of their bounding.

Little Owl heard them coming and quickly climbed a tree. Gray Bear turned to face them, shaking his bow threateningly since he had no club. He spoke fiercely, in a low voice: "Huh! Dogs stay back. I am a warrior!"

The dogs halted their rush and began to circle him at a respectful distance. Camp dogs have lived under a simple dictum since the earliest days: The dog that attacks an armed man is likely to be killed.

Now that Gray Bear's presence had been detected, his next move was dictated by custom. A single man or the leader of a party, approaching a strange camp, stands and hails the camp, then waits for an answer. This he did but there was no answer so he began to move forward again. He was expecting to see a shelter of some kind in the place he was approaching but there was only the rough face of a rocky bluff coming into view beyond the trees. Coming closer, he saw a large hollow which receded darkly under ledges of rock, seemingly the entrance to a cave. There was a fireplace, a circle of blackened rocks, just inside the entrance.

His interest became intense. What kinds of people were living here in a cave? He thought of the tales of the Little People, the Ancient Ones, who lived in caves and wore robes of bird feathers, but of course that was only a grandmother's story. Old men tell of the things that have actually happened to them during their long and active lives, but old women tell the oldest tales of all. They tell the stories their own grandmothers told to them when they were children.

Gray Bear hailed the camp again. He called out, "Come out and talk. Send one man out to talk to me!"

Time passed. The dogs grew bored with watching him. They stood or sat in a loose circle around him. They had stopped growling and were yawning, scratching and snapping at flies. Finally their leader, a huge black dog with a yellow face and chest, trotted away into the forest. The others leaped up and followed him. Then suddenly there was movement in the mouth of the cave. A man was coming out.

He was a very thin, ancient looking man, walking slowly on legs that seemed to be made only of bone with no muscles under the skin. And his arms were also thin and weak looking. The man's face was like a skull with skin stretched over it. His cheeks were sunken, the cheek bones jutting out strangely. But he was grinning in a friendly fashion and lifting his weak right hand in the gesture of peace. His only garment was a dog skin draped about his waste. He carried no weapons but the thing that caused Gray Bear to bristle with a desire to fight was the man's hair. It was long and hung down to his shoulders. No man of a friendly people wore his hair in this manner. Only the foreign western men who came from time to time as raiders wore their hair long. Gray Bear gripped his bow, the only weapon he had, and drew an arrow from his panther-skin quiver. The man showed no fear, only continued to grin and make the sign of peace. This put Gray Bear in a quandary. Perhaps it was dishonorable to shoot a man who was so weak and helpless. He notched the arrow but did not point it. The stranger raised his hand in the sign of peace and then began to make the gestures of the silent language which is known to all people. He signed, "Name—mine—Thunder—Far—much—sick—much—hungry.

Gray Bear felt impelled to answer; "I—Gray—Bear—Big—River—People—Big—Canoe—People—Why—you—here?

The stranger was raising his hand to make a response when his attention was diverted by the appearance of Little Owl. An expression of wonderment spread over his face as he stared past Gray Bear at the newcomer.

There was cause for his wonderment. Little Owl was wearing a buckskin shirt which hung down to his knees. This garment was covered with painted designs among which owls, bats, moons and stars were recognizable. There were other mystery symbols which no ordinary person would be able to interpret. The shirt bulged hugely around his hips with things that were being carried underneath. The eyes of the stranger darted from one young man to the other as if questioning how these two could be together. Gray Bear, of course, was dressed simply in the summer garb of a hunter or warrior. His shoulders and chest were bare, except for the carrying straps of his weapons. His deerskin sleeping robe was tied about his waist and hung down over the fringed leggings that all the prairie woodland people wore to protect their legs from the blackberry and other, thorns. His moccasins were the sturdy, long trail type, heavily sewn and lacking decorations. His head had been shaved except for a tuft of hair on the crown that served as attachment for a few turkey feathers which he hoped to replace soon with a crimson-dyed eagle feather, the symbol of a proven warrior.

Little Owl came forward speaking in a foreign language which Gray Bear did not understand. Apparently the stranger did not understand it either. He began making the gestures of the sign language again. Repeating his name and complaining of his hunger.

Little Owl drew a bag of trail food from under his shirt, opened it and handed it to the stranger who, without another word, sank down into a cross-legged sitting position on the ground and proceeded to cram his mouth with food. He gulped it down so rapidly he began to make choking sounds and then started to cough. Gray Bear was staring at him with disgust. In an angry voice, Gray Bear protested, "He is an enemy! We must either kill him or make him a prisoner. Why are you feeding an enemy?"

Little Owl responded cheerfully, "You cannot win he honors of a warrior by attacking such a weak man. I am going to feed him until he is strong. Then you can fight him and win the honors of a warrior. Unless, of course, if he becomes too strong. Then he will defeat you and win a red feather for himself." Little Owl was grinning as he spoke but Gray Bear saw nothing humorous about his words.

Gray Bear turned his attention to the mouth of the cave. He said, "You can talk to the spirits. Ask them if more men are hiding in that cave."

Little Owl tried to look fierce. He said "See how brave I am! I am calling on the spirits to watch me and see that I fear nothing" He marched right into the cave and disappeared in the darkness. Gray Bear stared after him, surprised.

Little Owl was pleased by the darkness of the cave. It seemed to fold around him like a black blanket protecting him from the chilly dampness of the air. He had always been fascinated by places like this. He had discovered this cave the day before, but the presence of the dogs had kept him from exploring it. Dogs always treated him with disrespect. They seemed to know he was not a warrior. All afternoon he had lain up there on top of the bluff above the cave, watching the stranger, making sure he was alone. The direction of the wind had favored him and the dogs had not become aware of his presence. But in late afternoon he had received a fright when the dogs leaped up suddenly and began to bark. Later he had decided they were barking because Gray Bear had passed on the windward side of the cave about three arrow flights away, following an ancient trail beside the river. But he had not seen Gray Bear at the time and had not learned that he was near until he heard his screams in the night.

Now, in the cave, he heard water dripping up ahead in the darkness and, not wanting to get wet, knelt down on the sandy floor where he was. He knew there were bats sleeping in the cave. He had seen them flying out at dusk, and was sure they had returned before sun rise. He began to sing.

> "Watchers in the darkness,
> with your wings of leather.
> Know that I am Monkon.
> Know I am your brother."

The sound of the singing resonated in the cave, booming in his ears, an effect that delighted him. He raised and lowered his tones, seeking the ones that caused the loudest effect. Outside the cave Gray Bear and the stranger listened with awe. It sounded as if a whole chorus of singers were howling in the cave. The stranger was so impressed he stopped eating. Gray Bear moved farther away from the cave. He expected the singers to come out of the cave and attack him. Finally he clapped his hands over his ears to shut out the evil sound and muttered, "If my brother comes out of there alive and unharmed I will treat him with respect. I will call him by the honored name, Monkon!"

# Chapter 5

## *The Cry of a Monster*

In the evening of that day they sat around the fire at the mouth of the cave. The breeze seemed cool after the heat of afternoon and the croaking of the frogs proclaimed that nothing dangerous was moving along the shores of the near by creek. They feasted on fat turkey hens that Gray Bear had shot earlier in the day.

Soon the stranger, full of turkey and good will, gave evidence of wanting to talk. The young men sat and watched him make the signs of the silent language that is known to all men. They watched attentively because they had been taught to listen to the words of their elders. They knew that if a man has lived for a long time in a world full of dangers, he must know many things that are worth hearing.

The stranger gestured gracefully with his big, bony hands. He made each sign carefully so that there could be no doubt about its meaning, but, even so, the sign language is not suitable for a long narrative. He signed, "Ground—belong—my people—far—far—there." He pointed to the northwest. "Sun—go—sleep—long—day—moon." Little owl understood this to mean, "in the direction there where the sun sets in midsummer." Gray Bear looked puzzled. The stranger continued, "There—much—grass—trees—small—There—much—wind—There— People—heap—brave—People—heap—strong—Earth—lodge—people." It was too much for Gray Bear. He continued 'to watch because a warrior is polite even in conference with an enemy he intends to kill when the conference is over, but his thoughts were on the next day's hunting.

Suddenly the stranger, leaning forward with the effort, uttered a loud, bellowing sound like that which might come from a large animal. Gray Bear started up in surprise as though he had been napping. Little Owl turned to look at him with an amused expression on his face. Gray Bear's face grew hot with embarrassment. He was angry with the stranger and glared at him with narrowed eyes. He muttered aside, to Gray Bear, "What was that noise? Why did he make that sound?"

Little Owl said, "He was boasting about the war cry of his people. He says it fills enemies with fear. I see that is true!"

Gray Bear ignored the gibe. He said, "That was the roar of a large animal. But I do not believe there is such an animal. I have never heard it or seen it."

Little Owl responded, "I know about this animal. You should know about it too! It is called the great gray bear. It is much bigger than any other bear. Its den is in those far mountains where the sun goes to rest each day. Sometimes it comes down to the land of our brothers, the Kanzas. They take its skin and wear its claws around their necks. But surely you should know abut this bear—it is the one for which you were named! After hearing this, Gray Bear sat there quietly with a dreamy look on his face. He had always thought he was named for the common black bear, an old bear, grey with age. He wanted to believe this thing about a bigger bear that he was named for. Hw wanted it so much it did not occur to him that Little Owl might not be telling the truth. At last he had a totem worthy of the strongest warrior. He tried to picture what the bear would look like when he saw it. Would it be black, or brown as common beers sometimes were? He tried to imagine the words he would say to it when they finally met. He imagined what it might say to him with its deep, rumbling voice. Now he wanted to leave this place and march to the land of the Kanzas as soon as possible.

But Little Owl was determined to stay where they were until the stranger was ready to travel. He had his reasons for this but he did not try to explain them to Gray Bear. Instead he told Gray Bear that the spirits would tell him when to march on to the west and to not do as they said would be sure to cause the failure of their mission. The big warrior grumbled about this but he remembered that he had promised to show respect for "Monkon"

So they remained there by the cave for what Gray Bear would consider a long stay. Soon they settled into a daily routine in which each did what he liked best to do. Gray Bear roamed the nearby woods and prairies for most of each day. He usually returning with a turkey, several grouse or other small game to roast over the evening fire, but the real purpose of his wandering was to watch for unfriendly strangers who might appear at any time in this dangerous land. Little Owl also roamed each day but stayed near the camp. He searched for medicinal plants, strange fungi and other items with magical powers known only to a shaman. In camp he spent his time chanting doleful songs, carving an ugly mask, and blowing foul-smelling smoke from a medicine pipe. The stranger, whom they now called Hungry Man, devoted himself to eating, sleeping, and trying to tell long stories by the evening fire.

His story telling was mostly a wasted effort. The gestures of the sign language required thoughtful attention and Little Owl soon became bored by what he recognized as the usual boasting of a warrior about past deeds. Gray Bear, still deeply suspicious of the stranger, made little effort to understand him. He expressed disbelief in all his tales.

By the time of the next moon, the stranger had undergone a remarkable transformation. The aged man with legs and arms like sticks, who had shuffled out of the cave on the morning when they found him, now had the appearance of a man of forty winters. His cheeks had puffed out with fat. His Ribs had disappeared. His arms and legs were round and his belly bulged like that of a bear in autumn. He proclaimed himself a warrior who had counted many coups against strong enemies. He had three wives, he said, and nine children. But Gray Bear declared this man was too weak and foolish to be a warrior and surely no father would have allowed his daughter to marry such a person.

On their last night by the cave Little Owl stood by the evening fire and made a formal speech: "Ho, listen to me; hear important words. Grandmother Moon has told me it is time for us to leave. When we came here she was the Moon of Yellow Flowers. That is the moon when nights are warm. Warriors can travel far wearing little clothing. They can sleep on the ground without the need of heavy blankets or a fire. But only two more moons are good for travel. Then it will be the Bucks-fighting Moon. Nights will be cold and leaves will fall from trees. We must complete our journey and return to our home before the land is hidden under snow. So listen to my words: We will leave beneath tomorrow's sun!

His eloquence was wasted on the audience of two. Gray Bear was resentful that his brother had assumed the right to say when they should leave. Certainly that was the duty of a chief, which he intended to become. And he didn't like being told things he already knew, such as how the seasons change and moons are named. He growled, "I wanted to leave this place long ago"

Hungry Man understood nothing Little Owl had said and believing it was his turn to tell one of his stories, he began to wave his hands in the gestures of the sign language. He did not seem to mind that no one was watching him. He continued until his fellow campers lay down to sleep. After that he sat there by the dying fire mumbling to himself in his own strange language.

# Chapter 6

# *The Trail West*

Next morning Little Owl directed Hungry Man to construct travois, to be pulled by his dogs. These, of course, consisted of long poles, their front ends attached on either side of the harness of a dog, their trailing ends dragging on the ground. A crude platform of sticks lashed across the dragging poles could carry as much as a man could carry on his back but they relieved a man of such a burden, so that he was ready to defend himself if attacked by enemies. Gray Bear disapproved at first since these contraptions would slow their march. He repeated his earlier argument that Hungry Man should not be allowed to travel on with them but should be abandoned to take care of himself or starve. His protest was futile. Little Owl wanted a travois to carry all his magic gear. He spoke to gray bear for a while, after which the proud, would-be warrior, changed his mind and expressed the opinion that since managing travois dogs was something even a child could do, Hungry Man should be able to do it. The foreign man was delighted to hear of his new duty. Now he could carry all of the food he had been hoarding. and, best of all, he no longer had to worry about being left behind to starve.

When the morning sun had climbed half way up the sky Gray Bear strode away toward the river. He had scouted all around the cave many times and knew how to find a main trail to the west. He was accompanied by the leader dog, the one called Yellow Face. This dog had become accustomed to following him on his hunting and scouting forays. Now it ran ahead, searching with its magic nose and ears for the same signs Gray Bear sought with his roving eyes. Behind him came the two travois, one behind the other, each pulled by a single dog. Hungry man followed behind the second travois, walking on tender feet, and perspiring profusely in the summer heat. Little Owl came last, lagging far enough behind to avoid the dust raised by the dragging poles. He was glad to be alone now with his thoughts and often chanted a ritual song, softly of course, to the rhythm of his footsteps.

By the third day of travel Gray Bear had become disgusted with the slow pace of his companions. Recklessly he left them, jogging tirelessly in the relative coolness of morning accompanied by the equally tireless dog. As the morning passed the west wind grew in force, cooling his face and his bare chest as he jogged. The faster dog ran on ahead and waited for him in shady places under the trees. It was a fine thing to have that dog scouting his path. Gray bear had no doubt that it would warn him if enemies were nearby.

Hungry Man, following with their travois, was pleased that Gray Bear had disappeared. He plodded along, occasionally shouting at the dogs to slow their pace. Those dogs seemed to take an idiotic pleasure in their work, lunging in their harness and sniffing eagerly at the trail as if in anticipation of some reward just ahead. Little Owl had fallen far behind. He was digging up some precious roots he needed for a magic potion. He saw no need to hurry. He had noticed that Hungry man was limping and was confident that Gray Bear and the dogs would warn of any danger.

Now Hungry man had slowed even more as the trail passed through pleasant shade in a streamside forest. Sunbeams, coming down through openings in the leafy canopy, became bright shafts in the swirling dust raised by the dragging poles. Hungry man's eyes were squinted almost shut against the brightness and the dust. He was longing to sit down in the shade and rest but he was afraid this would displease Little Owl. The thought of an angry shaman helped him to ignore his painful feet. He was going along, reluctantly, closing his eyes from time to time, when he received a sudden surprise.

Just ahead, an evil thing had moved onto the path and was sleeping there. Lying in a patch of sunlight, surrounded by the shade of the forest floor, it seemed to glow in unnatural, angular patterns of orange and yellow. It did not look like anything alive but resembled a painted ceremonial mask, weird and frightening in appearance.

The first dog stepped right over it, ignoring it, as if it had no odor and made no sound. The dragging poles passed by on either side and it awoke. The second dog passed on one side of the apparition and the tip of one travois pole bounced right over its patterned back. The colors began to swirl and writhe in the patch of sunlight. The eyes of the demon were clouded because it was soon to shed its skin. But the two deep pits in its horrid face were sensitive to heat and allowed it to focus with unerring accuracy on any warm blooded thing, on a deer mouse, a ground squirrel or, in this case, a hot sweaty foot of Hungry Man. Twin daggers stabbed and Hungry Man grunted with surprise and pain. He stood there staring at the angry snake as it crawled away. He saw at once that it was not a rattlesnake. It was a kind he had never seen in his northern homeland. There was a growing pain in his bitten foot. He suddenly felt cold even though the day was hot and his face was dripping perspiration. And, worst of all, fear of the unknown possessed him. Surely an evil spirit had struck him, putting a deadly medicine into his foot that was going to kill him! He sank into a crouch in the shade of a tree and began to chant a dying song. There was fear in his voice. It rose in a plaintive wolf howl.

"Oh, the sun will go down.
Oh, the hungry wolves will come.
Place my body high in a tree.

Oh, the sun will rise,
The vultures will come,
Wrap me in a tough bison skin.

Little Owl heard him and hurried up the trail. He didn't have to ask what had happened. Hungry man was making signs, explaining his misfortune, as soon as the shaman came into view. He even managed to describe the snake well enough for the shaman to identify it.

Little Owl set about preparing the proper potion to treat the wounds and began chanting a medicine song. His chanting could hardly be heard as Hungry Man had started howling his dying song again. He felt it was necessary to complete this ritual of his own before he became too weak to sing.

"Oh the winter winds will blow,
Oh, the warming sun will come.
Take my bones down from the tree.
Oh, the summer days will pass,
And the leaves will fall again.
Take my bones back to my lodge.

Little Owl knew there was little chance that the bite of a copperhead would kill a grown man. Especially one as fat as this one, he thought with secret amusement. He remembered that his aunt, a woman noted for her bulk and loud voice, had been bitten by a copperhead while gathering fire wood near the village. She had gone on with her work, ignoring the pain as stoically as a warrior and loudly expressing her scorn for snakes that are weak in spirit. But he did not tell Hungry Man that he was in no real danger. He preferred to have his patient believe that his life had been saved by the skill of a medicine man.

Soon after the sun was at its highest Gray Bear sat down to rest in the shade of a big oak tree. The dog was there to guard him, so he shut his eyes and soon dozed off into refreshing sleep. When he awoke, he was amazed to see his brother standing over him. Little Owl had a prankish grin on his face. He said, "Ah, if I were a Pawnee warrior your scalp would have been easy to take.

Gray Bear was not amused. He said, "If you were a Pawnee, my dog would have warned me and I would have your scalp." But he was angry with himself for having been surprised and even angry at the dog though it was understandable that it had given no warning of the approach of a familiar person.

Little Owl told him what had happened and that they must go back and wait for Hungry Man to recover before they marched on. He did not mention what kind of snake had bitten the foreign man. It was better, he thought for Gray Bear to assume, as he no doubt would, that the Great Spirit Rattlesnake, the one that can kill a strong warrior, had done the biting. Then he could claim for himself the honor and respect due to a shaman having great healing powers.

Gray Bear was very angry. He declared, "I will not go back. Why must we be burdened with that worthless man? He is not a good person. He does nothing useful. He eats too much. He tells big lies. Ho, it is well known that snakes bite liars. Their forked tongue is the symbol of a lie. Real warriors have a straight tongue. They never lie and they watch where they are stepping. You can go back if you wish, I am going on. If you are wise you will go with me. We do not need those clumsy travois. We only need one dog, this wise hunter who runs with me everywhere."

Surely such a long speech from the usually taciturn Gray Bear indicated how angry he was, but it had no effect on Little Owl. He was looking right into the eyes of his brother and had started to murmur a magical incantation. So of course they turned back.

Now Little Owl led the way and Gray Bear followed. He was frustrated, hopeless and angry. They went now with the wind blowing on their backs. Gray Bear knew, and Little Owl should have known, that a wise hunter or warrior does not march in this manner, his scent carried before him, warning all the creatures down wind of his approach. But Gray Bear, though he was a wise hunter, had surrendered his will to the shaman and responsibility for their safety to the dog that was up there scouting in advance. It was sniffing the wind with its magic nose, but the wind gave it no knowledge of what was ahead.

Soon they approached a place where the lush herbs and grasses of the summer rose up to mingle with the leafy branches of trees at the edge of a forest. Back of this screen, fifteen big warriors were crouching, ready to leap out onto the path. Some held bows with arrows already notched, some gripped big clubs of yellow wood. All were perfectly still; only their eyes moved and gleamed with cruel exultation like the eyes of a bobcat fixed on a doomed bird.

# Chapter 7

## *Captives Become Guests*

Yellow-face was scouting ahead, his magic nose sniffing, his keen ears erect. But his nose brought him no hint of what lay down-wind before him and the fierce warriors lurking at the forest edge stilled even their breathing as the dog passed. After he passed he was down wind from their hiding place and their foreign scent came to him. He wheeled and dashed back to Gray Bear. Growls rumbled in his chest and the fur on his shoulders stood up in a ruff.

The warning came too late. A chorus of screams came from the forest edge—shrill cries that seemed to express the terror that would paralyze their victims. The brothers stood like statues as the big warriors sprinted from the woods and surrounded them. No blows were struck, but the strangers were expressing fierce threats, waving war clubs, pointing arrows, and pantomiming the taking of scalps by pretending to clutch a shock of hair with their left hands while the knives in their right hands slashed at an imaginary head.

It seemed to Little Owl there was nothing that could save him. His eyes were flared wide. His mouth was gaping. He actually moaned with fear. He shut his eyes to avoid the sight of the ferocious faces and seemed to feel already a tugging at his hair. His scalp crawled and he cringed in expectation of the scalping knife. In his imagination, always creative, he saw himself lying dead here in this place tonight with opossums feeding on his body.

Gray Bear folded his arms in front of his chest and forced his features into an expression of haughty disdain. He seemed to be looking far away, over the heads of his tormentors, as if he were examining the clouds for signs of rain. His act of unconcern was not difficult. He had recognized familiar ornaments and tattoos. These were kinsmen from the big town by the Marsh of Swans. They were panther clan warriors, many of them too young to wear a feather. He knew that this was only a rough game, one in which he had participated many times with the boys of his own village. His only surprise was that the big dog was pressed against his shins, growling defiantly at the threatening warriors. A quick glance revealed that some of the fierce scowls were about to lapse into boyish grins. He had heard the moan of fear from his brother. He was disgusted but he hissed a warning. "Don't let them see you are afraid!"

Little Owl's agile brain came back from the darkness of terror and began to focus on the problem at hand. He too now perceived that these were kinsmen. He felt a wave of relief that he was not going to be killed. He felt shame about that sound of fear that had escaped him. He hoped no one besides Gray Bear had heard it. Then he felt a surge of resentment that he, who was going to be an honored shaman with the title of respect "Monkon," was being subjected to this childish persecution. His resentment grew at once into real anger. He would show these childish warriors who and what he was!

He turned slowly until he was facing directly toward the leader, a huge man with a crimson-dyed eagle feather dangling from his scalp lock. He stared right into the leaders eyes. This is a thing a warrior does not do unless he intends to kill the object of his stare. But of course the rules of behavior are different for a shaman. Then he reached under his robe with his good left hand and brought out the ugly mask he had been carving. He donned the mask, with a sweeping gesture, and then spread his arms, lifting his robe on either side until it was like two broad wings. On his chest there was a shining ornament of copper in the form of a bat with wings extended. He had now assumed the ritual pose of a bat shaman. The noisy strangers fell silent. Even the dog ceased its growling and Gray Bear turned and stared at his brother, actually allowing an expression of surprise to replace the stoic expression he had assumed. But the greater surprise was still to come. The bat shaman folded his wings so that they concealed his chest, then opened them wide again and a live bat fluttered in front of his chest for an instant then flew away, darting off erratically as a bat is likely to do when disturbed in the daytime. Startled exclamations burst from the watchers. Some of them actually stepped back as if to distance themselves from this powerful medicine man.

Little Owl removed his mask and addressed the leader. "Ho, you will call me Monkon. You need not fear me; I recognize you as brothers. You and I have the same grandfathers. We have the same enemies. I came here to visit the medicine men of your big town. I want to share my wisdom with them." He gestured toward Gray Bear and said, "This boy is my follower. He goes with me because I need someone to kill game and scout ahead for enemies. As you have seen, he has much to learn about scouting for enemies. Perhaps you will let him join in the warrior games and practice for war. Everyone knows your people are the greatest warriors in the world. The two of us have been together since we left our village by the Great Smoky River. No one else is traveling with us. This big dog that you see here is important to us. Only he knows how to find a secret place beyond the land of the Pawnees where I must go before the end of summer. You must protect him from the dogs of your town. I have finished speaking."

Gray Bear knew he should now speak. But his anger had surged with the remark that he had done a poor job of scouting ahead for enemies. And how could he speak without calling his brother a liar? These warriors must be told about Hungry Man who was undoubtedly an enemy of their people. They should be warned that he was lurking nearby. And he knew nothing about some secret place to which they were traveling. He was going west to see the huge bear for which he had been named. And he was also angry because Little Owl had called him a boy and his follower! So he stood there raging inwardly and saying nothing.

The leader of the warriors began to speak. He introduced himself, saying his name was "Deer Stalker in the Forest Where the Deer Hide At Night" He was a chief of the panther clan." He greeted "Monkon" with a show of respect and invited him to the town that lies at the center of the world. He assured Monkon that a shaman of that town would be glad to have him as a guest. He bragged that his people are respected for their hospitality as much as they are feared by enemies. "Now this young man who wants to be a warrior can stay in my lodge. He will go every day to play strong games and practice fighting with other young men of his age. And we will try to keep this brave dog from attacking the dogs of our town." He grinned as he said this last thing so everyone would know it was a joke, but he had called the dog brave. His people always admired bravery, even in a dog.

Soon the whole party was marching away in single file. Little Owl walked at the head of the column just behind the chief. Gay Bear was at the rear with other young men who had not yet won their feathers. The dog followed him so closely its furry shoulder nudged his leg from time to time. It was still suspicious of the strange men.

They followed a faint trail which went across the bison meadows where sweet-smelling grasses waved, shimmering in the hot sunlight. Sometimes the trail led through shady woods, where trees grew near the banks of brooks or creeks. Sometimes they walked by, or through, groups of grazing bison that were not disturbed by their passage, except for an occasional bull that turned to face them as they passed. It was not the season for hunting bison and the men were careful not to alarm the big animals as this would make them more difficult to kill in the great fall hunt. Deer dashed away from their path, white tails flashing alarm to others of their kind. A big bull elk stood and watched them pass. It showed no trace of fear.

Though still disturbed by the things his brother had said, Gray Bear was already feeing proud of being with this fine party of men. Marching along, he dreamed of accompanying them in some exciting adventure. He vowed they would not find him wanting in courage or skill in the use of weapons.

# Chapter 8

## *The Great Bat Spirit*

In the long summer twilight the people gathered around the fire in the central place of the town. They spread buffalo robes on the smooth ground of the meeting place and sat on them, cross legged. The summer air was scented with burning oak, the familiar odor of home and safety. The fire snapped and crackled. Bright sparks flew up into the sky as if eager to join the stars that were beginning to appear. Firelight played on the pale, dome-shaped lodges and the tops of the trees beyond them. They listened patiently to long speeches by their leaders. Each speaker stood facing the place where the chiefs and important warriors were seated with the firelight reflected readily on their faces. The people listened intently as if expecting to hear something of importance. But most of what they heard was not new or different from the things they had been told in the past.

Finally a medicine man came to the speakers place. He had a fierce scowl that seemed to be permanently set in the deep lines of his face. The robe that was draped about his shoulders was made of an untidy assortment of animal skins. It was hung with curious trophies and amulets as well as feathers and the tails of small animal. His head was covered by a bulky mass of turkey plumes. Gray Bear thought he was the ugliest and most untidy person he had ever seen. He was disgusted by the sight and disturbed that he could scarcely understand what the

43

man was saying. The voice was hoarse and raspy and there were words he had never herd before, words that people did not use in their daily speech. But he did understand the man's repeated warning about the dangers which are associated with darkness. He reminded them that they were the children of the sun and that they were protected always by the shining god who rose each morning in the east in answer to their prayers.

He ended his speech my making some mysterious motions during which a struggling bird appeared in his hand. No one knew where it had come from and there were murmurs of surprise in the audience. Then he tossed the bird into the air and it flew about, flashing as red as blood in the firelight. It circled in the lighted area around the fire, than flew off into the darkness.

There was a stir among the people as they began to talk to one another expressing their admiration for the shaman. Many of them had already heard the story of how the young visiting shaman had produced a live bat, the symbol of darkness, in the bright sunlight earlier that day and they perceived that their own shaman had responded to that magic act by producing a redbird, the symbol of day and sunlight, here in the night.

When they became quiet again, the panther chief who had brought Gray Bear and Little Owl to the town stood up and described again the events of the afternoon to the crowd. Then he asked the visiting magician, whom he described as a young man from a Down River Village of their kinsmen, who had already earned the title of "Monkon," to come forward and demonstrate his power for the people.

Gray Bear was sulking again at the disgrace of being ignored, but he felt a sudden interest as he saw that Little Owl was carrying a long lance as he cane forward to the speakers place. He had never seen that lance before, and what was Little Owl, certainly a non-warrior, doing with such a weapon? It was not the sort of thing a hunter or warrior wants to carry as he goes stealthily through the river woodlands or crawls through tall prairie grasses, hunting for game or seeking enemies. Indeed, the main use of a lance is for dispatching bison that have been injured in their plunge from a high bluff during the great fall hunt.

The people around the place where Little Owl had been sitting had exclaimed with excitement as he stood up. Perhaps the lance had appeared magically at that instant. As he came forward he did not go directly to the speakers place but went instead to where the drummers were sitting at one side of the chiefs and important warriors. He spoke to the musicians and they seemed to be agreeing to whatever it was he said to them. He then went to a position quite close to the central fire. He stood there, holding his lance upright, until the crowd became still, then a bit longer while their anticipation grew.

Suddenly he startled everyone by uttering a shrill, wavering cry as if he were calling to someone, or something, far away. He repeated the cry several times, pausing, with his head cocked as if expecting an answer from the darkness. The people were listening too but they heard only the distant howling of coyotes. After his last cry, little Owl turned to stare at the darkness over the nearby lodges as if he had heard a response to his calls. The people stared toward the same place. Some only rolled their eyes as if afraid to turn their heads. The women and children were beginning to look frightened. The warriors looked very stern as they did when they were trying to look unconcerned.

Next Little Owl began to dance slowly around the fire. He chanted in a deep voice, like the beating of a drum, and the musicians took up the rhythm. They beat their drums softly so they did not drown out the sound of his voice. The biggest drums sounded like thunder in the distance. Gray Bear recognized the chant. It was the one the whole chorus of spirits had been chanting inside the cave on the morning they found Hungry Man.

From where he sat, Gray Bear could look directly across the fire at the face of the Old Medicine Man. The man was staring at Little Owl and there was such a look of murderous hatred on his face that

Gray Bear reached involuntarily for the handle of his axe and gripped it tightly. That man was looking at Little Owl the way a warrior looks into the eyes of an enemy he is desperately trying to kill.

Little Owl danced and chanted for a long time. The fire was dying down but when a woman came forward with wood to replenish it, he motioned her away. Soon after that he gestured to the musicians to cease their drumming. Now he was drifting around the fire in complete silence. He was holding the lance near its blunt end, reaching up as high as he could into the air above. And he was staring upward so that soon all the people had their heads tipped back, gazing at the sky. That was when the bats came. Suddenly they were there, fluttering around the tip of the lance. It seemed to Gray Bear that Little Owl was shaking the lance, very slightly, and that its tip was blurred and difficult to see. When this happened the bats darted at the tip of the lance, one or more of them of them actually striking the point, as if biting it. They repeated this behavior several times while Little Owl shifted his hold on the lance, slowly lowering it until the bats were circling not far above his head. The people murmured their surprise and the bats flew away. Immediately after that Little Owl raised his arm slowly and pointed at the dark wall of trees down by the river. In a trembling voice, a voice that expressed awe and wonder, he began to chant again:

"Look there! See him! See him standing! See the great bat spirit standing! See his wings spread out to cover, all the lodges by the river. See his big ears listening, hearing. See his great mouth gaping open, see his sharp —".A woman screamed with mindless terror. The whole crowd erupted with howls of fear. Feathered warriors sprang to their feet shouting and pointing. Some whooped war cries and waved their weapons as if trying to drive the apparition away. Gray Bear saw nothing, but next to him a warrior exclaimed, "Wah! It was as big as a lodge! It could swallow a whole buffalo with that mouth!"

Whatever was there, it could no longer be seen. The shouting and wailing gradually died away. Gray Bear heard a man nearby demanding that the bat shaman be killed, at once, so he could not call the awful monster back again. A calm voice was calling for order. It was the old medicine man, the one who had been glowering with hatred while Little Owl performed. He was by the speakers post calling for the people to be seated. When he had their attention he assured them that people who pray to the rising sun each day have nothing to fear from the spirits of the night. He reminded them that the spirits are always watching, so why should they be frightened by the sight of one of the mysterious beings? He also assured them that he, Monkon, would protect them from any spirits lurking in the darkness.

Gray Bear heard warriors assuring one another that they had not been afraid. Some of them actually laughed derisively at the idea that they could have been frightened. Soon the people were quiet again. Children stopped their crying. Even the dogs of the town that had been thrown into an uproar of barking became quiet. A favorite story teller came forward. He stood by the speakers post and started telling a fascinating tale of a far quest, of lurking enemies, of how clever warriors outwitted their foes. This was a favorite theme for story tellers.

When the meeting was over, Gray Bear went with his hosts, the family of the chief, Deer Stalker, back to the lodge where he had been provided with food and a bed. These people, who had chattered happily on their way to the evening fire, were now strangely quiet. To Gray Bear it seemed that they had a new attitude toward him because of what his brother had done. Was it respect, suspicion, or fear? He could only wonder.

# Chapter 9

## *The Daughter of the Chief*

Gray Bear had begun a new life here in this big town, one that suited his nature perfectly. Each day he went to the practice field to engage in rough games with companions of his own age group. In addition to a vigorous and sometimes painful team sport in which a hard ball was knocked about with sticks, they competed in running, in wrestling, in shooting arrows, throwing hand axes and other warlike activities. Sometimes they went on scouting forays, pretending to search for enemies, or practiced creeping up for a surprise attack on an imaginary village. Though all they did was practice for war they were treated with respect and admiration. Old warriors knew their names and greeted them in a friendly manner. Small boys followed them about admiringly. When they passed a place where women were working, shy maidens covered their mouths with their hands to hide self conscious smiles.

It was not that the people were fond of war. Every morning they prayed for peaceful days, than spent their peaceful day preparing for war. Young men must devote their time to becoming strong and determined warriors. Fierce enemies lurked to the north and south, and to the east and west, who longed to possess this rich land here at the center of the world It was a land where corn grew tall and pumpkins grew large, where herds of bison feasted on the tall grass, white tailed deer browsed at the forest edge and bears fattened themselves in preparation for their long sleep in winter dens.

As the days passed, Gray Bear felt himself becoming stronger and more agile. Though he usually displayed bruises or felt aching muscles in some part of his body he was aware and proud that his shoulders were bigger, his arms and legs more powerful, and that he had become a respected person. He had not yet earned the coveted red feather but he believed he was the equal of any man who wore it.

Meanwhile another new interest had come into his life. Not long after his arrival in the lodge of his host he had become aware that the eldest daughter of the Panther chief, a girl of perhaps sixteen winters, was beautiful. She had large bright eyes, softly rounded cheeks, and a shapely mouth that always seemed about to spread into a smile. She walked gracefully with her long black hair that was always beautifully combed swinging in rhythm with her footsteps. He thought to himself, she is the kind of woman that will be given in marriage to a chief or important warrior. And this was followed, quite naturally, by the thought "I am going to be a distinguished warrior, soon I hope."

Though it was forbidden by custom for a male guest to look with interest at the women of his host's household he found himself stealing quick glances at the girl as if some mysterious power had taken control of his eyes. He struggled against the impulse to look at her and felt his face grow hot with embarrassment whenever he thought someone, especially her father, might have noticed where his rebellious eyes had wandered.

So far Deer Stalker showed no indication that he knew his young guest was developing an interest in his oldest daughter, but there were signs that his discourtesy had been detected. He sometimes noticed the two younger daughters looking at him, then giggling together about something. Worse yet, the fierce looking old woman who was the assigned protector of the oldest daughter seemed to spend much of her time glaring at him whenever he was present. Well, let her glare, he had the warrior's skill of keeping his face expressionless and surely a man was not required to keep his gaze straight ahead at all times.

Then came the evening when his bowl of food was brought to him, not by one of the wives of his host, as was usual, but by the girl herself. He had been sitting with his eyes cast down, as was proper at the approach of a woman, but suddenly he recognized the beaded moccasins and the familiar ankles below the fringed skirt. Shocked, he threw his head back and looked up into the face of the eldest daughter. The girl had been bending forward, offering the bowl, looking down at the top of his head. Since the fire was behind her, her face dimly lighted by reflected light from the lodge wall, and she made no attempt to control her expression. And her expression was warm and friendly, faintly smiling. Their eyes met. He felt a peculiar tension in his eyes as if they were straining to see her better. Perhaps she felt the same for hers had flared with surprise. She ducked her head and quickly backed away. He sat there staring straight ahead, trying to look as if he had not even noticed the girl. The other people around the evening fire seemed unaware that anything unusual had happened, except for one. He shot a quick glance at the girl's protector who was standing back of the seated men on the other side of the fire, and sure enough, that fierce old woman was glaring at him as if he were a Pawnee prisoner she was preparing to torture. He maintained his stern expression for some time, than realized he was holding a bowl of food in his hands. How long had he been sitting there as if he were refusing to eat his host's food? That was a really serious discourtesy. He felt his face grow hot again with embarrassment and he began to eat very fast. Across the fire, the ever-watchful old woman was looking at him with an expression of knowing and disgust. He managed to gulp down the rest of the stew before someone came to take the empty bowl. Soon, one of the little girls, the youngest of the three sisters came to take the empty bowl away. She was small, perhaps nine years old, not yet subject to the conventions that regulate the behavior of adults. She was looking at him boldly as she approached. As she took his bowl she bent her head close to his ear and whispered something of which he understood only two words" "Mina" and "husband." Then she turned and dashed away. Gray Bear's heart bumped so vigorously he thought the people sitting nearby would hear it. What had the little girl said? "Mina" was an honorary name for the oldest daughter. Had Mina told her to say something? Was this only a childish prank by the little girls? In his confusion he had to fight to keep his expression calm, to pretend that nothing of importance had happened.

# Chapter 10

# *The Warning*

It was the time of sunset again. Gray Bear was walking slowly toward his lodging place—slowly, because he enjoyed this time alone with his thoughts. He was composing a song as he went along, softly singing words he would not have wanted a chance passer-by to hear. "Ho, you are slim, yet strong like a panther. You are as clever as the little wolf that sings at night on the prairie. You are as soft and warm as the fur of a bear cub." No, he would not have wanted any of his manly companions to hear him singing words like those.

Someone stepped out of the woods onto the trail just ahead of him. The person was wearing the robe and mask of a shaman. It was his brother, Little Owl. Gray Bear felt a sudden surge of anger. He was ready to say no to whatever was going to be demanded of him. And sure enough, when Little Owl spoke his first words were a command.

"Ho, you must get ready to leave this place. We must go tonight. Listen! After the fires have died down I will call to you from the river. I will repeat the call of the barred owl three times. You will rise from your bed and come prepared to travel far.

Gray Bear responded angrily. "Huh! I will not do this thing. I will not leave now. Soon I will earn a warrior's feather. You go where you wish. It is no concern of mine!"

Little Owl was staring right at his face with narrowed eyes. A warrior does not look into the eyes of another unless he is planning to kill him. But a shaman does not have to follow this rule. His voice hissed with emphasis as he spoke, "Do what I say brother and you will still be alive when the next moon comes. If you do not do this thing, you will die tomorrow. Hear me! That old medicine man, the one who does childish tricks with redbirds, has ordered his bear clan men to kill us."

Gray Bear glowered at his brother and said, "I have many friends who belong to the Bear Clan. I do not believe they are planning to kill me. They were my friends today, how can they be enemies tomorrow?"

"Hee!" said Little Owl. "I am telling you what I know. That old man, whom foolish people call "Monkon, has discovered that we were traveling with that foreign man from the western lands. Some boys who were playing along the river found him hiding in the place where I left him after I gave him the powerful medicine for the bite of that deadly snake. They tried to take him prisoner but they were too small. Some Bear warriors were summoned to that place to kill him but he was no longer there. They studied the tracks on the ground and they could see that you and I had been there with him. Orders have been given for tomorrow. We will be seized and bound. We will be tortured to make us tell why we were sheltering a dangerous spy. Then we will be killed! The spirits have told me what will happen. We must leave tonight!"

Gray Bear had a very angry look. He said, "Why did you not tell them about that man? You should have told the truth to those men who captured us. You lied to them. You said we were traveling alone. You pretended to be the leader. You did all the talking. You said I was your follower. You called me a boy! Now I will go and tell the chief, Deer Stalker, about this matter. He will advise me if there is danger."

Little Owl was contemptuous. He said, "Hee, I know what he will say. He will say why did you wait until now to tell me about this foreign spy? Ho, you waited until you were in danger. You are afraid now. That is why you are telling me this. You deserve to die."

Gray Bear shoved his brother aside and went on along the path. He did not believe he could be treated as an enemy. He was sure Little Owl had made up the story because he needed a strong person to protect him as he traveled on into the dangerous western lands.

His anger cooled as he became certain that no one wished him harm here in the big town. People he met on the path greeted him in a friendly and respectful manner. Some passing women, old enough to be his mother, stared unabashed at his big shoulders and powerful arms and smiled admiringly. It was easy to believe that all was as it should be here in this big town where he had felt he belonged. He trusted the companions with whom he had been practicing the skills of a warrior. He trusted his own strength to fight anyone who might want to harm him.

Somebody was running down the trail as if coming to meet him. It was a slim person, running fast. He stopped in astonishment when he saw who it was. The oldest daughter of Deer Stalker came dashing up to him, stopped and began to speak. Yes, she was actually speaking to him! His astonishment at this unthinkable behavior was so great he at first did not grasp the meaning of her words. She repeated: "You must go away. Bear Clan men are coming after tomorrow's prayers to kill you. You must go away tonight. I have prepared a pack for you to carry. It has food, a sleeping blanket and some of my father's arrows. My father knows about this thing but he will not tell you to go away. He will not tell a guest to leave. He says this thing is an insult to his honor. He says he will stand beside you and fight the bear men. I think you will both be killed. I will have to put ashes on my head. Maybe I will cut off a finger as some women do to show their grief." Her voice broke with a suppressed sob as she continued, "I will cut off two fingers."

Not until later did he grasp the full significance of what she had said. He was staring at her face. She was more beautiful in the light of the setting sun than in the light from a cooking fire. He said, "What is your name?"

She looked at him with surprise. She said, "Ah?"

He repeated, "What is your name?"

She had had a look of tenseness and worry, then of grief. Now suddenly gentleness came to her face. She looked away, shyly, her eyes down. When she spoke, her voice was as pleasant to his ears as the song of a wood thrush at sunset. She said, "My name is Shining Light.

He repeated her name, "Shining Light." His own voice sounded strange to him. It was like the voice of a grandfather speaking to a small child. "It is a fine name. But it is not a panther name, ah?"

When she answered, her words were like a song.

"When the big cat, In-ge-thon-gah,
Prowls around a hunter's night fire,
gazing at the flames in wonder.
His fierce eyes shine like two torches,
in the darkness of the forest"

Then, wonderful to see, she smiled at him, saying, cheerfully, "I am named for the light that shines in the eyes of that panther."

She darted past him and ran off up the trail.

He shouted after her, in a voice hoarse with emotion, "Shining Light! You will be my wife!"

He heard more footsteps coming along the trail, fast steps, as if another person were running to meet him. He turned to see the old woman, the girl's protector, coming along with rapid, short steps, leaning forward as if about to fall. She was clutching a large knife in one hand. When she saw Gray Bear was looking at her, she began to yell threats in a shrill voice. Suddenly, he wanted to laugh. He stood there grinning at her until she was close enough to slash at him. He dodged the knife easily, sprang off the trail and disappeared into the woods.⸽

# Chapter 11

## *Gray Bear Departs*

Now he was in the lodge of his host, Deer Stalker. Night had come and the two men sat beside a small fire that lighted the interior of the lodge. A woman came in with two bowls of food. Only this one woman, who looked old enough to be Deer Stalker's grandmother, was there to serve their food. She went out, muttering angrily about not being allowed to sleep in her customary place. Gray Bear did not feel like eating, neither did Deer Stalker. But courtesy required Gray Bear to eat and required Deer Stalker to join him.

When the food was finished Gray Bear spoke. He said, "I will bring no trouble to your lodger. When the fires are out in the town I will go away quietly."

Deer Stalker waited a long time to respond. Perhaps he was trying to decide what to say. Perhaps he wanted to stand beside Gray Bear in the morning and fight the bear clan men. Sometimes a seasoned warrior would rather die in a brave fight than simply continue to grow older. But finally he spoke. "You have decided what you will do and that is good. A man should decide what he will do and not wait for others to tell him what to do."

After another silence he spoke again. "It is my sorrow that I have no son. If you were my son, I would be proud. I have watched you in the games. I have watched you practicing with your weapons. I have listened to your words here in my lodge. You are as quick as a bobcat. You are as strong as a bear. You do not say foolish things. It will not be long before the bear clan men forget what they are supposed to do. Their medicine man, Long Claws, has done evil things. I know men who say he will not live much longer. They say this with angry looks on their faces. When he is gone you can come back to my lodge. You be treated as my son. You will be a panther."

Gray Bear was surprised. He felt very proud. And he felt sad for this big man who had befriended him, and who was sad because he had no son. But then another thought came to trouble him. If he were the son of Deer Stalker, even an adopted son, he could not marry Shining Light. A man cannot marry his sister. And no one can marry a member of the same clan. That has been a law since the oldest days of the people. But that was a problem which could wait until later. He said, "Father, you have made me very proud. I will not forget what you have said."

After that they were both quiet for a long time. The fires of the big town were dying. The night was becoming very dark. When they went out of the lodge, the big dog, Yellow Face, rose up from his sleeping place in front of the lodge to follow Gray Bear. The two dog-companions, though they were afraid of Gray Bear, were ready to go wherever Yellow Face might lead them. Deer Stalker led the way, following a path that soon passed along the edge of the greet marsh which gave the town its name. Soon it seemed to Gray Bear that they were almost clear of the town. But they had to pass one last small lodge. It was occupied by a solitary old man, an unimportant person, one who had never become a warrior. He lived here with a large number of half-starved dogs. Now those dogs that had been sleeping around the lodge came barking fiercely at the dogs of Gray Bear. Soon it sounded as if all the dogs of the town were barking and dashing to the scene.

Yellow Face and his two followers rushed, with ferocious growls, to meet those hostile dogs. Deer Stalker unlimbered his war club and hissed a command at Gray Bear, "Go! Run! Follow this trail!"

Gray Bear would have obeyed this chief if the command had been to leap from a high bluff or into a raging fire. He dashed away, running recklessly along the dim trail lit only by starlight. As he ran he heard the sound of the dogfight rising into high-pitched, frenzied cries of rage and pain. Dogs were killing dogs back there! He wondered if he would ever see Yellow Face again.

Glancing back, he saw that a few torches were beginning to flare in the darkness and he heard men shouting, but no dogs came barking after him. He thought that if none of the dogs were following him in the darkness, those men with torches might as well be searching for an invisible spirit of the night.

Soon he slowed his pace, knowing it was dangerous to run fast on a trail where he could not see where his feet were falling. There was little chance he was being followed now and he began to think about where this trail was going. It would go back to the place where the Osages had captured him and Little Owl. There he would find the river trail to the west, the trail along which Little Owl had followed him after Hungry Man was bitten by the snake.

Suddenly Gray Bear knew what he must do. He talked fiercely to himself as he ran, "I will find that long-haired man and I will kill him. I will go back to this town and I will stand beside the counting post of the bear clan. I will wave that scalp and I will say. "Look at this Bears! This is what I have done! Now no one here can call me an enemy. I have killed your enemy! I claim a coup for this! It is now my right to wear a warrior's feather!"

# Chapter 12

## *The Executioners*

As the sun climbed up to its high point in the sky, dark storm clouds gathered above the western edge of earth. Gray bear studied those clouds anxiously, knowing a rain would erase the tracks of Hungry Man that he was following. Ahead of him the dog, Yellow Face, was following the trail with his magic nose. The faithful dog was probably suffering with the wounds, gashes on his sides and shoulders and badly ton ear, that he had received in the fight with the other dogs on the night they left the town, but he bore his pain as stoically as a warrior and ran on and on through cool mornings and hot afternoons on the task his master had had assigned him.

Soon, with the dark clouds hiding the sky, the ground beneath the trees lay in an eerie twilight, but Gray Bear had come upon a well worn path and on its dusty surface were the foot prints of a man and two big dogs. The prints were so fresh the wind had not blurred their edges. Hungry Man was just ahead! Gray Bear dashed past yellow face and ran with powerful strides down the trail. He was running with his war axe in his hand, ready to strike.

But the storm struck first. High overhead a roaring wind began to tear the treetops. Limbs broke with loud cracking sounds and fell around him. The air was full of flying leaves. Gray Bear dashed on ignoring the danger of falling limbs. Then the rain came, big drops flying in the wind, drenching the surface of the trail, wiping out the foot prints. He stopped then, not because of danger or discomfort, but with the thought that the man he was following might have turned off the trail to seek shelter and that in the confusion of the storm he might run right past him. Gray Bear found shelter under a vine-covered tree and crouched there, wet and chilled, waiting for the storm to pass. The big dog that had been fearless when faced with the dogs of the town, and with bears and wolves on this journey west, crouched, trembling, against Gray Bear's shins apparently terrified by the noise of the storm.

The storm moved on toward the east and the rain stopped. Gray Bear emerged from the shelter and began to jog along the pathway that he had been following. His feet splashed in puddles and his leggings soon became dark with mud. But there were no fresh tracks for him to follow and no scent of smoke to indicate that Hungry man had stopped to dry his blanket.

Gray Bear looked back, hoping to see Yellow Face. With no scent to follow, the tired dog had dropped behind. The dog was not to be seen but after a while there came the sound of barking. Was Yellow Face trying to warn him of something? Gray Bear stopped and waited.

He soon saw the cause for the barking. A file of tall warriors came jogging into view. Each wore a crimson-dyed eagle plume attached to his head so it was free to twirl and flutter in the wind. Gray Bear's mouth stretched into a broad grin. These were his companions from the big town, young men he had trained with in the daily games. He murmured names of those he recognized,

"Big foot, Night walker, Small Bear!" And there was one older warrior, a famous one, called "Crazy Bear." It was clear that all of them were members of the Bear clan. As they came closer he raised his hand in greeting, but they did not respond. Instead they stopped half an arrow flight away and stood talking to one another. He was puzzled by their behavior but he started toward them, hailing them, "Ho! do you not know me? I am here following an enemy of the people. His voice faltered, his grin was replaced by open mouthed astonishment. Their leader, a haughty young sub-chief named "Growler", had made the sign that means "Kill him."

It was the ritual sign that a leader uses to order the death of an enemy, usually a prisoner who has been captured in war. That sign seemed more terrible than the words themselves. Gray Bear's mood changed instantly from pleasure at seeing his friends to the awareness of certain doom. He stood there, stunned into inaction while the executioners sprang forward with lifted clubs.

Sunlight was on his face. H was aware that Grandfather Sun was watching to see if he died bravely. Would Shining Light hear that he had been killed as an enemy of the people? Would she hear that he had died bravely? Now she would never be his wife.

The anguish of that last thought was transformed into a soaring rage. He raised his war axe high above his head as if preparing to throw it. This was a challenging gesture. "Cowards," he roared, Ten of you to kill one warrior! Growler, I challenge you to fight." Even as he said this he knew Growler would not accept the challenge so in the recklessness of utter desperation, he yelled, "Crazy Bear, I challenge you!"

They were around him now, but no blows fell. It could be that the chief had given another command. Perhaps they had planed only to test his courage. He shot a triumphant glance at Grandfather Sun. He knew his courage had been tested and he had earned honor, the kind of honor these warriors should respect. He was so elated he felt like leaping into the air. He looked right at the chief, Growler, and said, "Are you ready to die?"

Growler had a strange look on his face. A chief should not let his features betray what he is thinking. But, as Gray Bear knew, this was a chief who merited little respect. People said he was a chief only because his father was a powerful medicine man, the one called Long Claws.

Growler recovered quickly from his lapse in haughty aspect and said, "A chief does not have to accept the challenge of a mere boy who does not wear a warrior's feather. The great Monkon, my father, has ordered your death. We will also kill that boy, your companion, who pretends he is a magician. But since you have challenged our strongest warrior I think he should be the one to kill you. Crazy Bear kill this enemy of the people!"

Crazy Bear was a very big man and had a deep rumbling voice. He said, "I do not want to fight this young man. I am a killer of Pawnees not of small boys!"

There was laughter among the men. The idea that this youth with the broad shoulders and powerful arms, who stood taller than the hump of a buffalo bull, looked like a small boy to the giant Crazy Bear amused them. Someone said," Maybe Crazy Bear, is afraid to fight this small boy." There was laughter again, and Crazy Bear's eyes sought fiercely for the jokester who had dared to suggest he was afraid. The big man had more strength than several ordinary men but he had no sense of humor, at least not about his fame as a warrior.

Growler spoke to his men in a voice of command. He gestured toward a prairie swell that rose just outside the river forest and said. "Go there where Crazy Bear will have more room to swing his club. Also, out there, it will be easy for the vultures to find the body of this enemy of the people."

Soon the men were assembled on the knoll. The grass, grazed short by bison, was wet and slippery but that might make the fight more interesting. Crazy Bear still stubbornly resisted the idea of a fight. He repeated, "I do not want to fight this young man. Let Night Walker fight him. He is the same age and wears a new feather."

Night Walker spoke up at once, "He did not challenge me. Besides he was my friend. I do not think he should be killed."

Crazy Bear turned solemn eyes on the chief. "I think you should fight him yourself. He challenged you first."

There was a murmur from the men that sounded dangerously like agreement. Not one of them thought Crazy Bear was afraid to fight the youngster, but most of them were thinking Growler was afraid to fight. Growlers face was wet. He was perspiring quite unnecessarily in the cool breeze that had come after the rain. Trying desperately now to save his chief hood and perhaps even his life, he tried to shame the big man into fighting.

"Ho, Crazy Bear, everyone will be saying you were afraid to fight this boy! Ha, some are already saying you have done nothing since that day you got your name from fighting against the Pawnees. Yes people are laughing about the big man who was once a warrior!"

Crazy Bear was glaring with rage. Some thought that he was going to strike the chief. But instead he turned toward Gray Bear and growled, "I will show I am not afraid of this young man or anyone else."

Gray Bear was standing by himself near the center of the knoll. He was limbering his arm, as if preparing to throw the war axe. Now that it seemed he would have to fight Crazy Bear, his friend, Night Walker, came over to him and handed him a longer war club. But it was not nearly as large as the one Crazy Bear was carrying. Gray Bear thanked his friend, but laid the club on the ground He knew there was no way he could parry blows with the giant. He would use his own smaller axe. He had discarded his moccasins knowing that his bare feet and toes would give him a better grip on the wet ground. Soon the fighters were facing each other about ten paces apart. The older and more experienced warrior should have waited for the untried youngster to make the first move, but crazy bear was letting his anger guide him. He suddenly rushed forward, swinging his huge club. Gray Bear leaped aside and the club finished its swing in empty air. Crazy Bear whirled about, seemingly dragged by the momentum of his club, his feet sliding on the wet grass; he wobbled for a moment like a man losing his balance on slippery ice. Gray Bear did a surprising thing. He leaped forward and jabbed the big man in his side with the axe, doing no harm, just touching him and then leaping away. A chorus of approving exclamations came from the watching men. Gray Bear had counted a coup. To touch a foe in battle and then leave him unharmed was considered the most daring feat of all. The angry giant heard the sound of approval from the watching men and his fury increased. Again he lunged toward his agile foe swinging a mighty blow. Again Gray Bear dodged and this time his light war axe seemed to lash like a striking snake, right into the face of the big man. This time some of the watchers whooped with admiration. For the time of several heart beats Crazy Bear just stood there, streaming blood from his mouth and nose and spitting teeth, then he charged, as if crazed with rage and pain, not at Gray Bear but at the watchers. He charged into the group swinging his big club in a wild arc, as if in re-enactment of his attack against the battle line of Pawnee warriors on the day when he had earned his name. The men scattered like deer before a panther's rush, whooping their excitement, some of them diving to the ground, than whooping their enjoyment of this dangerous game. Crazy Bear stood there where the men had been, swinging his big club back and forth, his brow deeply lined as if he were wrestling with a problem that was too deep for him to solve. Then, to the amazement of everyone, he threw his club aside and walked off toward the nearby river.

Now Growler, who had felt himself the targets of that mad rush, rose from the ground where he had plunged to dodge that terrible club and with an exaggerated air of arrogant unconcern shouted, "Seize the enemy of the people and bind him like a slave. We will take him back to the town and let the Chiefs decide what is to be done with him. It is better to let all the people see what is done to spies and traitors.

Most of the men stood where they were. There were mutterings of disgust and anger. But three men who apparently did not understand that Growler had forfeited his right to give orders, moved forward to obey his command. Gray Bear began to taunt Growler; calling him a coward. He stood there ignoring the men who were approaching him and just before they laid hold of him he hurled his axe at Growler. It was a good throw. It glanced off the left side of Growler's head, doing much damage to his ear. Growler fell to the ground and lay motionless.

After that Gray Bear fought, bare handed, against three warriors who were trying to overpower him. There was a tangle of thrashing arms and legs and much fierce grunting and hard breathing. And then an astonishing thing happened. A big wolf, or was it a dog? came dashing out of the trees, snarling fiercely and biting frenziedly at the legs of the men grappling with Gray Bear. The watching warriors exclaimed in surprise but made no move to interfere in the melee. One of the warriors broke away from the fight with Gray Ber and tried to strike the dog with his war axe. Gray Bear managed to deliver a well aimed kick to the man's backside that sent him sprawling. The dog, moving with blurring speed pounced on the fallen man and bit him repeatedly. The other men who had been trying to subdue Gray Bear sprang to where they had left their weapons and the dog dashed away into the woods. Gray Bear went to retrieve the axe he had thrown. Growler was crouched on the wet grass, holding his head. He did not look up and Gray Bear ignored him. The three who had been trying to subdue Gray Bear seemed to have lost their will to fight. They were bleeding badly from dog bites, especially the one who had fallen. The other men were looking at Gray Bear admiringly. He sat down on the grass and calmly put on his moccasins. He rose and without looking at his erstwhile attackers, walked away, going through the trees to the river trail that he had been following before the storm.

Yellow Face appeared and began to run ahead of him along the trail. He found no more evidence of the man he had been following that day, but just before dusk he heard footsteps behind him and turned to find Little Owl jogging along the trail, following him. The shaman was breathing hard as if he had been following for a long time. But he looked very pleased, either with Gray Bear or with himself, or both. He said, "Ho that was a good fight you had with that old, weak warrior. I watched from the trees and no one knew I was there. After you left those bear men marched away as if they were going home. They left Growler there to rest. I treated him with a magic potion that will keep him quiet until the vultures come. I took his eagle feather for you to wear. You earned it and he will not need it anymore."

# Chapter 13

## *Pawnees!*

It was dawn on the River of the West Wind People. The rising sun blazed in a cloudless sky. Outside the river woods the rolling plains stretched away to a distance greater than Gray Bear had ever seen before. He gazed at the far away line where the sky came down to touch the edge of earth. He wondered if a man could run that far in a single day. He knew he did not want to try. Throughout the previous day, as he had traveled, walking or jogging, to the west, accompanied by his brother and the big dog, he had felt a growing reluctance to continue. Now as they finished their meager breakfast he suddenly asked. "Why are we going along this trail where no fresh tracks can be seen? Even the dog knows hungry man has not gone this way.

Little Owl looked at him thoughtfully before he answered. "I know where Hungry Man is going. He told me where his home village is located. He said follow the Kaw River to the west and turn north on the trail beside the Bug Blue River. This is the way he would go to his home village. Soon we will see evidence that he has passed this way or, if we were traveling much faster than he was, we will have o stop and wait for him. We will do this when we are safely past the Pawnee lands."

Gray Bear said, ".I don't like going this way. I want t go back to that big town now. I have proved myself a fighter as good as any man. I think they talk about me in that place. They know I am the kind of

69

warrior they need to defend their town. No one there would dare to threaten me knowing what I did to Crazy Bear."

Little Owl had a very stern look on his face now. When he spoke he sounded like one who has important things to say. He said, "Ho Brother, you are thinking like a child now. You are thinking only about what you want to do. You are not thinking about what is the best thing to do. You are forgetting that this mission we are on is more important than what you want for yourself. You think because you fought and won against that big old warrior, Crazy Bear, you can defeat any warrior you see. Hee, back there in that town I told you, if you want to keep on living you must do as I say. I warned you that the men of the Bear Clan were coming to seize you but you did not believe me. Then you learned that what I said was true. Now I am saying again, listen to me and what you hear will keep you alive and make you a warrior, maybe even a chief."

He continued, "Listen, and remember what I say! A foolish man acts with rage about a thing that he will not even remember tomorrow. A wise man says, this is not a big thing. I will not remember it tomorrow. But the foolish man rushes into a fight and is killed because of a thing of no importance. But the wise man lives on, forgets the incident, and enjoys many more years of life. Another foolish man is told to sit, absolutely still, and watch for enemies. But after a while he is tired of sitting, he feels like moving. So he moves and the enemy sees him and kills him. Another foolish man knows he should not light a fire because enemies may see the smoke. But he is cold. He wants to warm his hands over a fire. So he builds a little fire, hoping his enemies will not see it. But they do, and they come and take his scalp. Do you understand what I am telling you? Listen! Hear me! Foolish people, children and animals simply do what they want to do instead of thinking about what they should do. A wise person thinks first, than does the thing that he should do, not the thing he feels like doing."

Little Owl continued to look at Gray Bear for a while. Perhaps he was hoping for some sign that he understood or even agreed with what he had been hearing. Finally, the shaman added, "Ho you only want to go back to that town because you want to be near that girl—Bright Light,—is that her name? Yet you know that to be worthy of such a woman you must first become an honored warrior. To become such an important person you must do as I have told you: Think what is the right thing to do, then do it."

Then he continued, "I agree that you should see and speak with that huge gray bear that you want for a totem. And if you don't see that bear as we travel across this land where it sometimes appears, you must perform a vigil. You know what that means: You must stay in a hidden place without food or water until a spirit comes to talk to you. The spirits have told me you will have a vision of that big bear and it will either become your totem or it will eat you. If you are brave enough not to show fear and promise to do what it asks it will become your totem. It is well known by wise people that such bears only eat cowards. When a coward meets such a bear on a trail, the bear rears up and growls. It is only telling the man that he has intruded into the territory that belongs to the bear. If the man is wise and brave he talks quietly to the bear and slowly backs away. The Bear understands then that the man is not a threat and it goes on with whatever it was doing before the man appeared. But if the man is a coward he yells with fear and throws his war axe or shoots an arrow at the bear. This makes the bear very angry and it rushes at the man and kills him.

Gray Bear said "I do not need to e told how to act when I see a bear. I have seen many bears and none have eve r attacked me." Of course he was talking about the common black bears that are numerous in his homeland. He did not know that the great gray bear would behave in the same manner as the common bear but Little Owl seemed to know.

Later that day they came to a place where a big river with almost clear water came down from the north and ran into the Kaw. Little Owl seemed quite pleased to have found this place. He said o Gray Bear, "You must swim the Kaw and see if there is a trail beside that other river. Hungry man told me the trail is on the other side of the river—the side toward the setting sun." He seemed to have forgotten that Gray Bear would resent any order that he gave him.

Gray Bear said, "This is not the right time of day to swim a river. The sun will go to rest soon and I will be wet and cold in my bed. We will wait until morning. Then you will swim the river. I will watch from this bank and see if you get across. That water is deep but you can get the help of your spirit friends and reach the other side safely."

Little Owl changed his approach at once. "Ho," he said, all warriors know how to get their weapons across deep water without damage. I am sure you have this knowledge. Also, you can swim much better than I can and when you get over there you can use your warrior's skill to scout the woods for enemies. You will have the dog with his magic nose and ears to help you. He would not go with me. He does not like me. He is a warrior dog and likes to be with a warrior.

Gray Bear recognized all this as true. He promptly stripped off his leggings and placed the pack of food he was carrying and his sleeping blanket in a hidden place among the bushes. After that he called the dog to him and proceeded to tie his moccasins to the top of the dogs head. Then he stood on the bank and shot a few arrows across the Kaw, watching carefully to see where each fell. He laid the rest of his arrows beside his pack and tied he empty quiver about his own head like a wide head-band. Then, calling the dog, he walked out into the river. He was carrying his bow in his hand, but just before the water became deep enough for swimming he took the bow in his mouth, crosswise, the way a dog might carry a long bone. He and the dog swam across, going in somewhat the same manner, holding their heads up out of the water. The dog paddled rapidly with all four of its paws as if it were running in the water. Gray Bear paddled with his hands much like the dog but kicked his legs powerfully in the manner of a swimming frog. When they arrived on the other side, Gray Bear retrieved his almost dry moccasins from the dog's head and went to search for his arrows.

He had a peculiar feeling that he had arrived in a foreign land. Perhaps crossing this river to its north side reminded him of crossing the Big Smoky River of his homeland. His people seldom went to the north bank except with organized war parties going to fight the fierce Iowans or the hard-to-kill Sauks. Now he knew he was going into the land of the Pawnees. His heart was thumping with a strong premonition of danger. But the danger, when it came, was on the bank he had left. Over there he suddenly heard the calling of magpies. He knew these birds were usually solitary but now the woods on the south side of the river where he had left his brother seemed to be swarming with them He concealed himself in bushes and stared across the river at the place where he had entered the water. Suddenly Little Owl dashed out of the woods over there, running like a deer. He soared off the river bank and landed in the water with a great splash. He disappeared under the water and a wave spread out from the place where he had vanished and crossed the whole river, arriving as a ripple just below the bank where Gray Bear was watching. That wave seemed to symbolize the disappearance of the shaman and Gray Bear watched it with growing concern. Little Owl had jumped into the river wearing his shaman's robe and presumably carrying all his usual possessions on his belt. He had certainly hot been properly dressed for swimming, particularly under water. Gray Bear had a superstitious notion that Little Owl had changed himself into a fish or frog and was crossing the river in such a disguise. But suddenly his head popped up in an unexpected place, down stream from where he had entered the water but not quite half way across the river. Gray Bear saw that his brother had his mouth opened wide and seemed to be gasping for air. It was not an encouraging sight but as he watched, the shaman sank under the water and disappeared again. Now Gray Bear saw some motion in the trees across the river. He froze into immobility, hoping to blend invisibly with the trees and bushes around him. Foreign-looking warriors came out of the trees over there and down to the edge of the river. Gray Bear had never seen their like before but he had heard them described many times by old warriors boasting of their adventures as they sat beside the winter fires of home. These foreign-looking warriors were Pawnees, the ancient blood enemies of Gray Bear's people, and they were painted for wear. They did not look across the river toward Gray Bear but were staring down stream at the place where Little Owl had briefly appeared. Now was a very bad time for him to appear again, but his head rose up above the water and again his mouth was open, gasping for air. Ten or so Pawnees quickly drew arrows from their quivers and sent them flying toward the head of the shaman. He ducked under again and this time he must either have been inspired to hold his breath longer than before or else had disappeared for good beneath the water. Meanwhile Gray Bear had notched one of the few arrows he had managed to retrieve and took careful aim at one of the enemy warriors. It was a remarkable shot, the arrow hit the Pawnee in his upper left arm (Gray Bear had aimed for his heart) although the distance across the river was almost as great as one could hope to shoot an arrow. The man howled with rage and charged forward, leaping into the river as if he intended to swim across and attack the one who had shot him. His comrades loosed another shower of arrows, this time aiming at the location from which Gray Bear's arrow had come. But Gray Bear had leaped to shelter behind a large tree an instant after he shot his single arrow. Now, as soon as the volley fired by the Pawnees hit the trees and bushes around and behind him he dashed out of his shelter and quickly collected a few undamaged arrows—arrows that could be shot back at his enemies.

After that he ran as fast as he could run down river to the place where Little Owl might come out of the water. To his surprise he found the Shaman standing in soft mud below the river bank. He had a stricken look on his face and when he spoke it was almost a moan. He said, "I am sinking into this quick sand, soon I will e buried here with my head under water. He sounded very sorrowful as though he had little hope that he could be rescued. Gay Bear seized the trunk of a mall tree with one hand and extended his other hand to Little Owl who grabbed frantically with both his hands at the arm and wrist that was offering him hope for life.

Exerting himself powerfully, the muscles of his arms and chest bulging under his skin, Gray Bear dragged the shaman out of the mud and water and deposited him on the river bank among low bushes. This was done with urgent haste, partly because back of them in the woods the dog was growling fiercely, presumably at an enemy warrior. Gray Bear dashed through the trees toward the sound and came face to face with a Pawnee warrior, the one who had charged into the river in rage after Gray Bear's arrow hit his arm. Neither Gray Bear nor the enemy had the proper weapons for hand to hand combat but the Pawnee did not let this stop him from charging forward shrieking with rage. What did stop him was the big dog that sprang forward to clamp its jaws on his ankle. The man fell and the dog released his hold on the ankle in order to pounce on his victim and deliver multiple bites just as he had done with the Bear warriors in that other fight a few days earlier.

Men were shouting in the trees over toward the river. It sounded to Gray Bear as if the whole enemy war party had crossed the river and was charging down upon him. It was no disgrace to run if one is hopelessly outnumbered. He shouted for Little Owl to follow him and dashed away, running north on the trail that lay beside the Blue River. But soon he decided it was not safe to follow this trail so he turned abruptly to the left, then charged up the long prairie slope toward the summit of the wind-blown rise which lay to the west of the river. There was no place to hide up there but he had suddenly realized the day was ending. The sun was already hidden back of the ridge and it would be dark soon. Little Owl, following behind him, did not protest this new course, even though he would have liked to stay hidden in the woods beside the river. Some instinct for survival seemed to tell him that his best hope to escape the Pawnees lay in following this powerful warrior who seemed to know what he was doing. Besides he had felt the power in Gray Bear's arms and shoulders when he was dragged from the mud and had appreciated, for the first time in his life, the awesome strength of a trained warrior. It was as if he were suddenly aware now that in maters of war he must defer to Gray Bear.

Gray Bear knew he was the leader now. He had the knowledge of how to fight or hide on the prairie. He knew a whole heard of buffalo could disappear from sight by running over a rise of the rolling land. He knew a hunter or warrior could lie prone on such a height and see the motion of game or plan how to evade enemies far away.

Dashing over the crest, he stooped low and turned to the right. Now they would run parallel to the ridge, keeping low so their heads would not be silhouetted against the sky. Curiously, the dog seemed to understand this strategy; he ran to their left, well below the crest. As he ran, Gray Bear studied the lay of the land, planning how they would confuse their pursuers until darkness came to hide them.

# Chapter 14

## *Gray Bear Meets Grizzly Bear*

When Gray Bear awoke the darkness of night still covered the land. But he saw the big white star with its steady light that comes at some seasons scouting the path that the sun will take when it rises. He murmured appropriate prayers inside his head but no sound came fro his lips. He glanced at his brother to see that he was still sleeping soundly, then took up his bow and the quiver with its few remaining arrows and crept quietly away into the darkness. This was a thing he had planned the night before, to be in the forest beside the river when the first light of day came. He had seen deer lurking there at dusk and he yearned for the taste of fresh venison. He had grown weary of their travel diet of parched corn and dried buffalo meat. He had suggested to Little Owl that they pause for at least one day so he could obtain fresh meat. Little Owl had been scornful about his childish wish for better tasting food, quoting from the lecture he had given earlier about foolish men who do what they feel like doing instead of following a more important plan.. He declared that warriors on an important mission do not turn aside to hunt because their stomachs ask them to do so. So now Gray Bear was creeping away quietly, not only because he was hungry for good food, but to demonstrate to his brother that he did not have to follow his orders. The big dog, having ears that were always awake, rose up and followed him.

When the sky was growing bright in the east he surprised a fat, young buck and brought it down with just one arrow. It was a good shot. He noted carefully where the arrow had struck, thinking of how he would tell about this when he again had someone to talk to—a fellow warrior or hunter who was interested in such things not a would-be shaman who had only contempt for the common skills of hunters and warriors. He skinned the deer and prepared both the hide and some choice meat for carrying.

He was sure his brother would be ready to share this fine food and if he had anything to say about the morning's hunt he would be reminded that they had lost no time from their travel, only the time that Little Owl had wasted in sleeping until the sun was well above the horizon. He had plans for that deer skin. He would make rawhide leggings to replace the ones he had lost back there at the Blue River when he had abandoned his old ones in order to swim.

He felt very good about this hunt and the fine deer meat he was carrying. Now he was walking through the prairie grass that had turned yellow with the drought of summer, breathing the cool, sweet-smelling air of morning. He saw a red tailed hawk flying high overhead and heard its shrill cry. A herd of antelope on a nearby ridge were looking at him with their big ears pointed to catch any sound he might make. Perhaps the sight of all those listening ears reminded him to sing. He started composing a song about his morning hunt.

Big deer standing in the willows,
Big deer hiding from my arrow,
Ho, I sent him just one arrow,
Flying straight and true it struck him
Flying like a hawk it struck him
Just one arrow and the deer fell.

He stopped and turned to watch the dog. It was chasing a big jack rabbit, a gaunt creature with big hind legs and long ears. It had the look of a completely futile chase as the rabbit was loping along, effortlessly, staying just ahead of the dog. The dog was running furiously, its red tongue lolling, its sides heaving with exertion. Why was the dog exhausting itself in this useless pursuit of an animal that could outrun any predator on the prairie? As he watched the dog and the rabbit disappeared over a prairie rise.

As he walked on toward the place where he had left Little Owl another curious thing came into view. In the tall grass and reeds of a prairie swale he saw a small herd of buffalo. The arrangement of the animals was unusual. They were standing in a rough circle, facing inward. In the center of the circle a huge hairy beast was rolling on the ground. At first Gray Bear believed it was a single buffalo rolling and tossing there in the grass, but as he drew closer he saw it was shaggy and of a peculiar shape. It was like a huge brown dog, groveling and rubbing itself on the grass as dogs sometimes do. The watching buffalo were moving slowly forward as if their curiosity was overcoming any fear they had of the strange creature.

Gray Bear also felt intense curiosity. He hurried toward the scene and soon was so close the nearest buffalo obscured his view of the creature they were watching. He began to circle the herd, trying to find a place for a better view. In doing this he disregarded the direction of the wind. Suddenly, there in the center of the circle a huge shaggy form rose up to an astonishing height. The buffalo fled from the scene, bellowing with fear. One of the cows rushed right at Gray Bear but he dodged her without taking his eyes from the enormous beast that was now standing on its hind feet, staring directly at him. Its eyes were small, almost hidden in the fur of its huge face. Its monstrous head was set on a broad shaggy neck that sloped directly into enormous shoulders. It stood with its great front paws hanging down in front of its rounded belly. Those paws were studded with long curving claws.

For an instant Gray Bear thought of a giant man wearing a bear mask. But as his heart pounded in his ears he gasped in excitement and with recognition. This was the great bear he had come so far to see. This was the great grandfather of all bears. But he had never dreamed it could be so big. Now as it stood here facing him, looking at him, it was standing two heads taller than the tallest warrior. The wind stirred its hair, and he saw that the tips of the longest hairs were shining almost white in the bright sunlight. Gray Bear seemed to be murmuring his own name with awe, "Gray Bear - Great Gray Bear!"

The monster made a peculiar groaning sound, then dropped down on all four of its huge feet and began to walk slowly toward him. He felt a strong urge to flee, but as he turned to do so the wind whispered in his ears and he saw the swallows dipping toward the grass that had been disturbed by the buffalos and he remembered that the spirits were always watching. So, though his whole skin crawled with terror, he faced the bear and stood as firmly as a tree. Now this thing would be decided. The bear, respecting his courage, would become his totem or he would die here, torn apart by its terrible claws.

Five paces from him, the huge bear paused and reared up again. It was so close its broad face loomed above him. Its mouth was slightly opened, giving it a slack and almost humorous look. Its face was streaked with scars and its ears were frayed. Gray Bear saw those marks left by old battles and thought, this is a warrior bear!

An unreal, peaceful feeling came over him. It was the feeling he was facing a spirit, a god, a being of enormous power. There was nothing he could do but accept his fate; whatever this awesome creature decided for him. But he felt he should speak. In a voice choking with emotion, his throat so tight the words had to be forced out - He said. "Ho, Grandfather. Do you not know me? I am the one who bears your name. When I was born, when my spirit came down from the sky, my father looked at me and spoke your name. Ho Woo! You were ancient even then, ancient but powerful as you are today. Ho, we are a people who respect age. Gray hair is more honorable than a warrior's feather. It is harder to get!

The bear was wrinkling its nose. It was sniffing audibly. Gray Bear knew what it wanted. Later, after many retellings of this story, he would come to believe that it had spoken to him, saying, "Hee, Grandson, that is a fine piece of deer meat you are carrying. Surely that is a gift you have brought to me."

Moving cautiously, Gray Bear placed the hind quarter of the deer on the ground and slowly backed away. He continued to murmur his admiration for the bear as it ambled forward. It sniffed at the meat and began to eat. It held the venison firmly against the ground with one fore-paw and tore the meat away from the bone with its big teeth as easily as Gray Bear would have eaten the soft fruit of a pawpaw. Gray Bear was thinking with regret that the piece of meat was too small for such a big bear. The bear seemed to agree. It finished the offering quickly, licked it lips with a remarkably long tongue and began to stare at him again.

Gray Bear placed the bundle of folded deer skin on the ground. The fresh hide was still moist and smelled of blood. He backed away, continuing to talk softly to the hungry giant. The bear scratched at this new gift and seemed confused. It pulled at the edge of the unrolling bundle. Perhaps it was searching for the meat that might still be inside. It wheezed and made soft groaning sounds as it clawed at the unfamiliar object. Suddenly it turned and began to walk away. Walking away on all four feet, It held its head high and dragged the deerskin over the ground. It went down into the swale among the reeds as if it had a resting place there. The swallows followed it, dipping down over the patches of crushed grass where the huge feet of the beast had caused small flying insects to scatter ito the air.

Gray Bear called to the birds, saying, "I am going now to find more meat for grandfather. If I see him again I must have another gift for him" He moved away then, jogging toward the river, toward the grove where he had killed the deer. He saw Yellow Face on a nearby ridge watching him. Soon the dog came, running very fast to join him. It trotted by his side, so close it sometimes brushed against his legs. It kept looking back toward the place where the bear had been. Deep growls rumbled in its throat as if it were trying to warn Gray Bear that the fearful beast might be following them.

# Chapter 15

## *The Warrior Bear Attacks*

When the sun was half way up the sky, Gray Bear came to the top of a high prairie rise. He and the dog stood side by side gazing out over a vast expanse of rolling grassland but there was no moving figure, near or far, that could be the one they were seeking. Little Owl had disappeared from their camping place while Gray Bear was away on his morning hunt. Perhaps he had been killed and dragged away by a cougar. Perhaps some mysterious shaman's business had caused him to leave their camp to seek the companionship of spirits Perhaps he had simply marched away to teach Gray Bear a lesson. The dog had trotted away from the campsite, indicating that it was following the footsteps of the missing Shaman. Gray Bear had followed it resentfully.

Gray Bear felt only anger that his one follower was no longer following. He said to himself, not too convincingly, "I don't care what has happened to him. I do not need him. He was like a foolish child that always questioned my commands." They went on down the slope, the dog leading the way, sniffing the ground. Far off, in the direction they were going, a wall of dark clouds was hiding the edge of earth. Gray Bear could not yet hear the thunder spirits of the approaching storm but Yellow Face was pointing his ears in that direction and looking back nervously at his master from time to time. After a while they came into the pale shade of willows that stood wilting beside a dry stream bed. Gray Bear decided it was a good place to rest. He sat down on the matted grass under the willows and shut his eyes against the glaring light. Almost at once his head sagged forward, his chin rested on his chest, he slept. The dog lay beside him but it did not sleep. It tipped its ears toward the low roar of the distant storm and trembled.

Gray Bear dreamed that he was in his fathers lodge. His mother was showing him some fine new leggings of soft deerskin that she had chalked to snowy whiteness. He put them on and they fit perfectly. She smiled at him and held out a new sleeping blanket. Then he was talking to his father, telling him about his adventures in the far off land beyond the Blue River. In the dream his father was standing upright, strong and well. His pretty sisters were there too, smiling at him proudly.

He heard a dog growling and awoke. Men were shouting in the distance and there was a roaring sound as if some large beast were growling at them. Gray Bear sprang up and stood for a while listening. The sounds were coming from over the next ridge and the dry steam bed formed a sandy path that wound off in that direction. Gray Bear began to run along that path in the direction of the sound. Yellow face followed, reluctantly.

Dashing along, somewhat hidden by the willows fringing the stream bed, he soon came to a place where the sounds were much closer, just over the ridge to his right. There was a deep gully coming down the ridge and Gray Bear ran up that channel, stooping low so that his head was hidden by the banks on either side. Near the summit the gully became too shallow to conceal him so he began to crawl through the thistles and coneflowers up to the top of the ridge.

As he crawled, he faced the dark, threatening clouds of the approaching storm. Now the clouds had surged upward to the middle of the sky. The sun was hidden from view and a peculiar greenish light lay on the land under the cloud. In the distance directly ahead the lightening flared, forming a pattern of fire like a branching vine, upside down, that connected the sky to the ground. The thunder roared. Gray

Bear looked back to see if the dog was following. It was nowhere to be seen. He crawled the last few body lengths to where he could look over the summit and down the next slope; there he saw an amazing sight. At a distance of less than an arrow's flight below him, a huge grizzly bear, perhaps the same bear that had confronted him earlier that day, stood with its back to him. It was facing down the slope, facing five fierce-looking warriors who had their bows raised, their arrows pointed. Gray Bear, from his position directly back of the bear, felt that those Pawnee warriors were pointing their arrows right at him. Although he knew they did not see him, their fierce faces, excited and taunting, roused in him a fighting rage. He felt a surge of loyalty toward this bear that was facing his own hated enemies. In a sudden surge of bravado he felt confident that he and the bear was more than a match for only five Pawnees.

The enemy men made a short threatening rush. They were pointing their arrows with the bows half drawn but they did not shoot. Gray Bear was thinking those puny arrows would be like insect bites to the mighty chest and enormous head of the bear. But suddenly the leader gave a shout and the men dropped down in the rough herbage of the slope. Immediately the bear rose up on its hind legs in an effort to see its hidden tormentors. The leader shouted another command and they all sprang up and shot their arrows at the exposed belly of the standing bear. Two of the feathered shafts flew past the bear. One struck the ground in front of Gray Bear and the other hummed dangerously by his left ear. The roaring of the bear became higher in pitch; it was now a roar of pain as well as fury.

Gray Ber leaped up and shouted, "Attack, Grandfather! I am here to help you! Attack, now!" He tried to make the same roaring sound the bear was making. He thrilled to see the great ber charge as if in response to his shouts. He shot an arrow at the nearest Pawnee, than dashed down the slope trying to join the bear in its battle charge. The bear was moving with a speed he could not match. It bounded down the slope as if it were a buffalo running at full speed. The Pawnees scattered, trying to dash out of its path. The bear could pursue only one of them at a time, and the one it chose might as well have stopped and waited, resigned to his fate. The bear overtook the man and towered up over him, its enormous paws with their terrible claws reaching. It pulled him, hugged him, against its huge chest and bit savagely at his head. Then it hurled him to one side and rushed after a second victim. Gray Bear stopped t look at the fallen man. He was amazed to see that the man had been scalped. He yelled after the bear, Ho, that was a coup! He dashed on, following the bear. But the second victim had dashed over the next ridge, out of sight and the bear followed him.

Suddenly Gray Bear realized that everyone had disappeared. He stopped and stood peering about for a short time, then suddenly became aware that he was a target for hidden enemies. This was confirmed an instant later when an arrow whizzed past his head. He turned and raced furiously back up the slope, zig zagging as he ran. Other arrows flew past him and ripped into the herbage up ahead. Approaching the crest of the ridge he threw himself down and crawled through the sparse herbage. Over the crest he rose and ran, plunging down the slope beside the gully, rushing at last into the cover of the willows beside the dry stream bed. He ran hard along the stream bed, racing past the place where he had rested and on until he reached a denser stand of willows. He decided to make a stand there. He crouched down; watching the trail over which he had come. Soon his pursuers came into view. They came jogging down the dry stream bed, following the tracks he had left in the loose sand. He counted four of them. Apparently they had lost only the one victim of the bear. Gray Bear was well hidden in the willows. He notched an arrow and waited until they were close enough for a almost certain shot. He took a deep breath and roared the new war cry, the one the bear had taught him. The storm was almost upon them and almost continuous booming of the thunder blended with Gray Bears roaring cry. Perhaps the thunder hid any imperfection in his rendition of the sound. On a sudden inspiration, Gray Bear raised the pitch of his voice and began to imitate the frenzied sounds of a wounded bear.

The Pawnees halted, reaching for their arrows, and as they stood for an instant Gray Bear loosed his arrow. He was sure he had hit one man, but all four of them turned and fled back up the stream bed.

Lightening struck with a blinding flash nearby and the rain began to fall, the kind of downpour that makes it difficult to see anything half an arrow flight away. Gray bear dashed out of the Willow Grove and raced furiously through the storm in the direction he had been marching before he stopped to rest. He continued to run through he falling rain, running toward the north-west, the way Little Owl led him on the previous days. He did not know if the Pawnees were trying to follow. He looked back from time to time but saw nothing through the curtain of pouring rain. Then, finally there was something moving back there. It was Yellow Face. The dog was running to overtake him. Soon Gray Bear changed his course, more toward the north He knew the rain had erased his own foot prints so that the Pawnees could not find him. But it had also erased any tracks that Little Owl have left—tracks that the dog could have followed with its magic nose. He wondered what he should do if his brother had disappeared for good. He thought he would simply turn back; giving up what would then be a hopeless mission, returning to the big town to face whatever threat was left with the bear clan. Or, perhaps he should go home to his own village on the big river first and wait there for a while before returning to the big town. But there would be a risk in that; a risk that Shining Light would be given in marriage to someone else.

On the previous day the brothers had been following the trail toward the north, the Big Blue River trail, that Little Owl had declared was the way to the end of their mission. Now Gray Bear came upon that trail again and began, reluctantly, to follow it. Suddenly he realized the tracks of Little, Owl were there on he damp surface of the trail. Little Owl was just ahead. Now Gray Bear really felt frustration. His chance to return to the big town alone had vanished. There, ahead, was Little Owl, not on the trail but off to one side, diligently digging up some mysterious roots and softly chanting a medicine song.

Their greetings, if they could be called that, were not cordial. Little Owl demanded to know why Gray Bear had left him alone in the camp that morning. Gray Bear disdained to explain why he had done so. The deer meat which was to have been the excuse for his early disappearance was of course gone and, incidentally, he was now very hungry. And of course he was too proud to ask his brother for one of the pouches of trail food, if any still survived after the shaman's disastrous swim across the Kaw River. So they went on up the trail to the north, not speaking to one another. Both were angry and discouraged.

# Chapter 16

## *The Voice of the Bear*

The nights were becoming cooler. Each morning the brothers awoke, chilled in their sleeping blankets of raw, un-tanned deer skin. The first touch of the morning sun was pure pleasure and by afternoon the land was warm again. The west wind played with the towering clouds as if it were still mid summer. The Grasshoppers seemed not to know that they were doomed by the approach of winter, they rattled as they flew from footsteps and the very voice of summer, the rasping of cicadas, still sounded from the brushy hillsides.

Gray Bear had developed a new habit. He talked almost incessantly as he went along. He told about his meeting with the great bear, how it had come to him and faced him, actually standing upright like a man. He exclaimed about how it had accepted his gift of food, had listened to him as he talked to it, and then of how it had appeared again, fighting beside him against the Pawnees and teaching him to roar its terrible war cry. At this point in his story he would take a deep breath then give a bawling roar, which really did sound much like the war cry of the bear. Sometimes' when he did this, Little Owl covered his ears with his hands and the dog slunk away in fear. When he was not talking he sang the song he had composed about the fight with the Pawnees, singing on and on, composing new verses, until Little Owl, seeking relief from the constant noise, reminded him that enemies could hear him from far away

When they were separated, mostly in early morning while Gray Bear went to hunt or to search for stones or wood for his weapons, Little Owl would practice roaring like the bear. He was always careful that Gray Bear was far enough away not to hear him. He had no plans as yet for how he would use the sound but he was always ready to acquire some new skill that might be useful.

One morning they came to the bank of a big river that neither of them could name. There was a well-worn tribal road beside the river, one of those trails traveled by whole communities of people traveling to new hunting grounds as the seasons changed. Only a few footprints could be seen in the smooth dust but they were of great interest. Little Owl studied them for a while then declared that the tracks had been made just before sunset of the previous day. He pointed out that the edges of the tracks had not been blurred by the strong wind of the previous day but tiny creatures of the night had crawled across them and dew drops falling from the trees and pitted them.

Gray Bear grumbled that he did not need to be told what he could see with his own eyes. He did not like to admit that his brother had the skills of a warrior as well as those of a shaman. Soon the tracks went down to the waters edge and into the shallow river where they disappeared. The Brothers went into the water themselves and waded to the other side. There was a smooth mud flat over there and the tracks were deep and clear in detail. The shaman called out excitedly, "Look at this! These are surely the tracks of Hungry Man. He has made new moccasins for himself but the feet that made these tacks are of the right size and I recognize the tracks of the dogs that are with him. He was Grinning broadly, probably in anticipation of his brothers reaction to the information he was about to give, He proceeded to explain that the foreign man must have traveled for all this distance without losing the two travois dogs that had been left with him in that place where the snake had bitten him.

"Ho, look at this! These are the tracks of the dog called 'Black Dog' and the other tracks are those of the dog called 'Scarred Back." He did not bother to explain that he had noticed, during their stay near the cave, that Black Dog had a front toe missing and Scarred Back had a damaged rear foot that left a peculiar track. "Yes, there is no doubt these are the tracks of Hungry Man!

Gray Bear was sneering. "Do you think I should remember the names of dogs? I did not know these dogs had names. Only very important dogs are given names, like the one who always scouts ahead of me and give warning if strangers are nearby. I call him Yellow Face because he has a yellow face and he deserves a name because he is a warrior dog. He has counted many coups!

Little Owl actually laughed at this, then said "Yes, he has counted more coups than any warrior I know!" Gray Bear looked at him, hard. Had his brother insulted him again? He decided to let it pass. He could criticize Little Owl for speaking more loudly than is customary when one is in foreign territory but as he opened his mouth to do this the shaman exclaimed,. "See the tracks of a third dog here! These are the tracks of the important dog called Yellow Face. He must have seen the tracks on this trail before you did and dashed ahead to greet his old followers!"

Gray Bear was stunned. Now he realized he had not seen Yellow Face since early that morning. Apparently the big dog had sniffed the scent of the other dogs and had dashed ahead to investigate. Gray Bear was embarrassed that he had not noticed the absence of his dog, but he quickly thought of an excuse. "He often runs ahead and waits for me in a shady place." He assured himself this was not a big mistake on his part and wondered why Little Owl had tried to make it sound as if it were important.

Little Owl turned and dashed off, following the tracks as if hoping to overtake the foreign man before Gray Bear actually saw him. Gray Bear followed, slowly, brooding deeply. His anger was directed mainly at the dog which had seemingly deserted him.

He was deliberately walking slowly, as if to indicate that he had no interest in finding Hungry Man. After what seemed to him like a long time, two figures appeared in the distance up ahead. It was Little Owl and a stranger who seemed to bear no resemblance to the man he had known as Hungry Man. Since they had no "friends" here on these endless prairies, Gray Bear was ready to fight. But as the two came closer he detected a faint familiarity about the other man that was at first puzzling and then increased his anger. The stranger came toward him with a friendly grin and his right hand rose in a sign of peace. His hair was cut short now, though in no recognizable style, and his very thin body was corded with muscle. Surely this could not be Hungry Man! Gray Bear remembered his resolve to kill this man and deliver his scalp to the Osages. But he had no weapons other than his bow and a few Pawnee arrows. For an honorable fight he needed a war axe. Besides, Little Owl was calling to him, reminding him that Hungry Man was a friend and had valuable information that they needed in order to complete their mission. So he kept his face expressionless and thought, this man is a fool. He will do something that will give me an excuse to fight him. Then I will take his scalp!

But Hungry man was no longer a fool. The long walk toward home had renewed his body and his mind. He had fled on sore feet from the Bear Men sent to kill him at the place of the snake. Walking west, he had alternately starved and found food on his own as the days went by. Finally he had noticed that his feet no longer hurt, that he felt strength in his legs and strength to use the new weapons he had devised to kill grouse, rabbits and finally a deer. He slept soundly at night and awoke every morning knowing that his strength had been recovered and that he was able to stride across the land like a young man. Sometimes, in the cool of morning he felt like running, sometimes he plunged into wide rivers, confident of his ability to swim to the other side. Yes, the days on the prairie, spent in moving as steadily as he could toward his far off home, had changed him from a soft man with too much fat on his belly into a powerful man who was fully aware of his new strength and confident of his ability to cope with whatever might await him on the trail ahead. The prairie had provided him with more food than he and his dogs could eat, with tall herbs and grasses in which he could seek concealment from his enemies and with high ridges from which he could survey the route ahead. . The bright sunlight had darkened and toughened his skin. The everlasting wind had cooled him in the heat of afternoons. Always he had his vision of home, of smiling wives providing him with all his needs, of worshipful children listening to his stories of adventures in far places, of fellow warriors seeking his advice about places and enemies. He reflected that during the past summer he had changed completely several times. In the beginning he had been a strong warrior, then an injured man, weak sick and starving, then a soft and foolish person dependent on others for his safety. He had been bitten by the terrible snake, than cured by the wise shaman, then a weak fat man fleeing for his life from strong enemies and finally a strong man and a warrior again. Now if he reached home again he would be a sage, a respected man of wisdom.

He knew the young warrior, Gray Bear, despised him and would look for a chance to fight with him, even to kill him. He had no fear of any man, but for the sake of his friend, the young shaman who had saved his life at least twice, once from starvation and once from the terrible snake bite, he would try to avoid any reason for a fight

# Chapter 17

## *The Long Journey Continues*

Still marching to the west, they came at last to where there were no trails of other men to follow. The grass was short, not even tall enough to hide a man's moccasins, and there was a growing problem with thirst as they could walk for half a day without finding a small stream or a slough with drinkable water. Now Gray Bear had a better reason for resenting the leadership of Hungry Man. Knowing the northern warrior could not understand his words, he spoke freely, expressing his resentment about having to follow the foreign man. Glowering at Little Owl he said," As I have told you, this man is too foolish to be a warrior, yet you have agreed to follow him and now we are so far from water we could die of thirst even if we turn back to that last stream we crossed".

Little Owl, tried to reassure his brother that Hungry Man knew where he was going and that another stream must be just ahead. This proved to be right, there was a stream, but it was small and had an ugly, reddish color from the clay soil over which it ran. Gray Bear refused to drink at first, but after another long diatribe in which he called both Hungry Man and Little Owl fools He threw himself down and submerged his face in the red water. After sucking up a drink that tasted like clay he had the look of a warrior painted for war and his appearance was even more suitable for the angry words that spilled from him. His anger was increased by the laughter of his two companions

Marching on, they came to a prairie dog town. It was the largest such town they had seen on their journey to the west. In addition to the small rodents that were standing upright and squeaking beside their dens or running about busily as if they had many tasks to perform, there was an unusual number of the large rattlesnakes that frequent such places. Little Owl had no concern about the snakes until he saw Hungry Man kick one of them out of his way. The snake quickly pulled its body into a coil, raised its whirring tail so that it pointed toward the sky, and buzzed a dire warning to the man who had disturbed it. Little Owl shouted at Hungry Man warningly, than signed to him to move on and not annoy the snake. After which Hungry Man paused to declare, in the gestures of the sign language, that he had no fear of snakes so long as he was accompanied by the medicine man that had saved his life after that other snake bite many days earlier.

Little Owl was shocked by this declaration. He knew there was little he could do for anyone bitten by one of these large rattlesnakes. He had pretended there was great danger from the bite of a copperhead and had made a show of administering a cure when Hungry man was bitten by that relatively harmless snake. But he was thinking fast, and he explained that the mysterious medicine which he had used to cure Hungry Man before had been lost when he was forced to swim a river, He was tempted to elaborate on this by claiming his impromptu swim had come about because of Gray Bear's failure to scout ahead properly after crossing that big river but decided against further speech—that is to say, more waving about of his hands in the gestures of the sign language. Both Gray Bear, with his newly painted face, and the nervous snake with its still-rattling tail, seemed to be staring at him suspiciously as he waved his hands.

Gray Bear said, "Tell him the snakes were put here by the Great Spirit to bite fools and liars. Of course Little Owl had no intention of saying anything that would offend the man who was now acting as their guide. He was glad Hungry Man did not understand the words of Gray Bear

Now Little Owl tried to turn the interest of his fellow travelers to another subject. He said, "These small brown owls that are living here among the lodges of the little animals seem to recognize me. That one we just passed stared right at my face and nodded its head several times. I don't know what these Owls are called. They are bigger than the small ones that live in the trees along the Big Smoky River—the ones that make the crying sound that the old women talk about. Yes, the women tell children that sound is the voice of a ghost warrior who was killed at night and must wander in the darkness forever crying like an owl. Now, I do not believe my father would have named me after such an owl. No, I think he must have seen these owls when he was a young warrior and traveled to this far off land. If so, I am glad he named me for these owls with their wise faces and their nodding heads. But I wish he had named me for a bat instead. I wanted to be known as a bat shaman before I earned the honorary name of Monkon.

Gray Bear would have chuckled at this if he had been in the mood for humor but he was still glowering angrily at his brother. It seemed to him that everything the shaman said was nonsense. It seemed to him his brother had no interest in useful things like stalking game or the use of weapons in warfare.

Soon they came upon another owl that stared right at the shaman, nodded its head as if in greeting, than ran into its den as he approached closer. Little Owl followed it to its den, then knelt down and looked into the dark tunnel where it had disappeared. He sprang up at once as the sound of a rattlesnake came from the den right where the owl had disappeared. He thought this was a remarkable thing—the owl and the rattlesnake sharing the same den and now the snake were warning him not to harm the owl. It did not occur to him that the owl could imitate the sound of a rattlesnake.

Another interesting thing happened as they were crossing the prairie dog town. In the soft dirt, recently thrown up by the digging of the rodents, Gray Bear saw the footprints of a bear. The prints were very large and he was sure they had been made by the huge bear he had encountered earlier. He wanted to follow the tracks and seek another meeting with his totem The tracks led off to the west toward the great hills where the sun goes to rest at night—hills that looked like dim blue clouds low down on the horizon. Gray Bear insisted that these hills were not far away and was determined to go there instead of following Hungry Man. It took all the persuasive skill of the shaman to restrain him from following those tracks. Only a promise that he would see the bear if he carried out a vigil, in a place soon to be selected by Little Owl, finally succeeded in turning him away from his interest in following the tracks. They went on to the north-west in the direction chosen by Hungry Man who was still intent on avoiding the Pawnee country by circling it to the west. Finally they came to a small river that was flowing across the short grass plains, probably one of the many tributaries of the distant Kaw River. Little Owl felt impelled again to point out that all these western rivers ran to join the river of their home —the Great Smoky River, Ne sho-d'say, The River of the Missouris. He said when their mission was finished they must find a raft, or even a canoe, and drift down these rivers to their distant home.

Now Little Owl noticed a stony ridge on the other side of the river. He declared he had been looking for this place. He declared the spirits had told him it would be the place for Gray Bear to stand his vigil. He said the spirits had promised that the Great Gray Bear would come to this place in as few days and agree to become the protective spirit of Gray Bear

Gray Bear felt an urge to sneer at this idea, but he remembered that he had promised to stand such a vigil and was thinking that it was a way to avoid following Hungry Man any farther. Also, if he agreed to stay here, he could do some morning hunts; have some good food and rest from his travels for a while. If Little Owl did not come back at the promised time he would be free to return to his home alone.

# Chapter 18

## *The Scaffold*

As Little Owl followed Hungry Man off to the north, he too reflected on the advantages of being free of a troublesome companion. Now he could think and plan as he went along without having to argue with the often troublesome warrior about what they were doing or why they needed a foreign man to show them the right trail. He looked forward to the nightly fire by which he and the foreign man could sit and talk by means of the sign language, giving their full attention to this basically unclear method of communication, repeating at their leisure those things that were difficult to understand, maybe even teaching one another words in their own diverse languages.

Hungry Man had told him that the young man, who had been the leader of the Elk River People when they had raided the village on the Smoky River, had been wounded in a manner that was certain to kill him. The wife of the old shaman, whom the warrior had killed during the raid, had shot a small bird arrow into the belly of the young chief. He said the young chief had denied that he was seriously wounded. He had declared, that his spirit was strong and that he could not be harmed by such a small arrow, especially one shot by a woman. That young man had worn the claws of the great bear around his neck and had declared that this powerful symbol would protect him and make him well again. On the journey home he had been very sick but he had tried to pretend he was not hurt. Finally his comrades had come, carrying him into the village as he was to sick to stand or walk. He had died soon after.

Little Owl had asked Hungry Man, bluntly, how he could know this thing since he had been separated from the Elk River Warriors shortly after the raid. Hungry Man answered without a moment's hesitation that he had encountered a scouting party of the Elk River People only a few days before Little Owl and Gray Bear had found him here on this far western trail. He said they had invited him to go with them just as that other party had done early in the summer. He chuckled at the idea, remembering that first invitation had caused him much trouble and he had no desire to repeat any part of it. But he had had a long talk with those Elk River men by an evening fire and had learned much from them.

After that Little Owl thought deeply about this new information. The young man's body would be on a scaffold on the burial ground of the Elk River People. Only a shaman could have had the new thought that came to him: "No man can go there, but a spirit can!"

Hungry Man was busy with his own thoughts as he went along. "This medicine man is my friend. He has done much for me. He saved me from dying in that far-off place where he found me. He saved me again from the bite of the deadly snake. He helped me to escape from the people who tried to make me a prisoner there by that river after the snake bit me. Yes, he is my friend; now I must help him in the way he asks. But why does he want to go to a forbidden place? That is an evil place, that hilltop where the bodies are of the dead are tied to high scaffolds underneath the sky. It is a place for crows and vultures, not for living men. Only a medicine man would want to go to this place and only for some spirit reason I do not understand. He wants to find the scaffold where the young chief lies. Surely he will not dare to touch the trophies of that warrior. Even he would not do that. Hungry Man shivered at the thought and put it from his mind.

Near sunset of the third day after leaving Gray Bear they came to a wooded hilltop and looked across to the next ridge, a barren ridge, where the burial scaffolds stood. Even from here they could see which one was new, which body still lay, full-sized, upon its platform, still protected by wrappings of tough bull hide from the horrible feasting of the vultures.

Hungry Man was eager to leave. He made a feeble excuse about the need to cross the river to the north before nightfall. He murmured a kind of parting ritual, in his own language, and then hurried away without a backward look. When Little Owl last saw him, he was running swiftly like young messenger carrying urgent news.

Little Owl stood for a long time staring at the scaffolds on the hilltop. He did not dare to go closer in the remaining daylight, knowing he would be killed at once if he was seen by the people who made use of this sacred place. Nor did he admit to himself that he would be going there in the coming night. There are some things a magician must conceal even from himself. When it was dark he lay down to sleep, wrapped in the bearskin robe which Hungry Man had given him as a parting gift. If there had been familiar watchers there, human companions or spirits, they might have remarked that he had, for once, fallen asleep immediately. Then, soon after that, they would have seen a mysterious, shadowy form which moved away, silently in the darkness toward the place of the scaffolds, leaving the bearskin, rolled on the ground as if a sleeper were still there.

It seemed to Little Owl that his spirit drifted effortlessly across the valley, then up the slope of the bare hill to the place where the night wind whined among the structures of tall poles. His spirit went among the awful shadows on the ground, feeling the air around it heavy with death. Does a spirit breathe? Is it troubled by unpleasant odors in the air? Does a spirit need the climbing poles that had been placed there so the bearers of the body could climb upward? The spirit used those poles.

Atop the scaffold it crouched for a while, staring out across the starlit landscape, hearing the coyotes wail. Then—how curious that the hands of a spirit should be trembling—it cut the thongs which bound the bull hide around the body of the enemy chief. Yes, it was strange that a spirit, a thing of thought, as weightless as a shadow, could hold a knife of glassy obsidian and cut through tough leather. And there, beneath the eyes of the spirit, bound to the sunken chest of the dead warrior, was the sacred medicine bundle of the Smoky River People.

There under the dark sky the spirit knew triumph. It took the bag into its hands, feeling the weight of memories—all of the memories of the people hidden in the bag. It was no longer alone. The spirits of the Smoky River People were all around. There was silent singing and the silent booming of big drums, a silent orison of victory.

And then the spirit felt a curious urge. It coveted the necklace of huge bear claws which was around the neck of the corpse. With a quick slash of the obsidian knife the cord holding the claws was cut. The silent drums ceased their beating. From the nearby forest came the screams of a dying bird which had been seized by some horror in the night. The spirit drifted back to the place where Little Owl was sleeping and placed the trophies beside his bed.

It seemed to Little Owl that he awoke immediately after his spirit returned from its mission. He was still wrapped in his sleeping robe but the sacred bundle was clutched to his own chest. He knew that it was real because the odor of death came from it. When he arose and moved away that odor went with him. It seemed to follow him like an evil spirit of the night.

He gathered up his belongings and fled. He thought to himself that his spirit had left no tracks on the ground and the people of this place, if they found the body had been disturbed, could not follow his trail. But another part of his mind was urging him to flee and telling him to go by water.

He went to the place that Hungry Man had told him about. A place where canoes were hidden. The Elk River people, ever ready for attacks by enemies, kept additional canoes hidden in secret places on nearby waterways. He found the ones by the creek which would carry him toward the place where Gray Bear was keeping his vigil. He launched a canoe and drifted away in the darkness. He was tired, but triumphant, not only about the thing which he—which his spirit had done, but also about his plan for the future which now seemed almost certain to succeed.

# Chapter 19

## *The Vigil*

Little Owl had told him to stay in this place. He had murmured the strange incantations that he had used on other occasions to insure Gray Bear's obedience. He had stared right into Gray Bear's eyes and swung the bat medallion on his chest back and forth in the rays of the setting sun. He had told Gray Bear, "This is the place where you will stay until the spirit bear comes. The spirits have told me you will dream big dreams here on this hilltop. Here your true totem will appear and talk to you." After that the shaman had gone away, following Hungry Man and leaving Gray Bear alone, as any man must be for this sacred ritual.

During the twilight of that day, Gray Bear found a flat place to sleep among the big rocks on the top of the hill. When he awoke next morning he moved to a sheltered place, shielded from the wind by a great rock that towered up higher than his head when he was seated on its sunny side. The morning sunlight was pleasant on his skin and a soft breeze brushed his face, lulling him into a pleasant drowsiness. But the day was long and the sun was still hot and his thirst grew until he could think of nothing but water. But the parting ritual of the shaman still had a firm grip on his mind and there was nothing to be done about this discomfort, so he closed his eyes and tried to go to sleep. Sleep did not come for a long time and when it did he dreamed of a broiling turkey hen with its fat dripping into the fire and a clear stream of water which disappeared when he knelt to drink. The hen, though thoroughly cooked, managed to fly away when he lifted it to his mouth and this brought disappointment and anger. In fact he was quite sure that Little Owl had stolen his food, but when he was fully awake he realized the medicine man was far away and the delicious food, for which his mouth was still watering, had been only a dream He slept, but poorly, opening his eyes from time to time to see the desolate scene. In the moonlight, rocks formed black shadows and straggly trees threshed in the wind. He heard the coyotes crying in the distance and then a deeper howl from nearby. This sent big animals, elk or deer, crashing through the brush down by the river. Their terror came right into his own mind. His hair rose but he fought against his fear. Almost awake, he clung to the dream, saying, "I want to stay, I want this dream." And back into sleep he sank, to face an awful monster in dream moonlight. An enormous wolf was there, before him, looking right into his face with gleaming eyes. It spoke! "Do you not know me? I am the spirit who is always near. When have I failed to guide you on your trail? When have I failed to fight the thing that threatened you? What other friend has stood before you as I have? When you die at last, as all men must, I will be there at your feet, facing your enemies until the end!" Gray Bear stared, face to face, with the big wolf. He had never seen a wolf so close before. Lit by moonlight it was dark in color and it had a pale face and head. It opened its mouth and looked at him, showing its long white teeth, but it seemed to be grinning. It was so close he smelled the odor of death, of all the things it had killed. But now he realized it was wagging its tail like a friendly dog! He awoke, and the wolf was still there, looking at him! He knew a moment of real fear. Then he realized it was not a wolf, it was Yellow Face! He thought, I must have been making strange sounds in my sleep and the dog came to see what was bothering me. He sat there looking at Yellow Face as though seeing him for the first time. He murmured to himself, "He is a fine dog. He is a strong companion. He has magic in his nose and ears. Ho, now I am a warrior of many symbols: The grizzly bear, the thunder spirit and the wolf. I will wear the claws of Great Gray Bear around my neck, I will paint the symbol of the lightning on my chest, and the spirit wolf will run beside me wherever I go.

It seemed to him his vigil was over. The spirit wolf had come and spoken to him! But Little Owl had promised the Great Bear would appear. Ha! Little Owl was wrong. He vowed to himself that he would have a good hunt at dawn. He would feast on the roasted meat of some animal and drink all the water he wanted. With that comforting resolve he shifted into a more comfortable position and closed his eyes to sleep. But sleep would not come. Surely, this dream he had had was just about a dog. Yellow Face had come up the hill to visit him, and had awakened him. Surely this was not the great dream Little Owl had promised. And he had promised Little Owl he would stay here until he returned. Such a promise, by a warrior, had to be kept. No, he must stay, after all. Sorrowfully he sat up and began to chant a mournful song.

The second day of course was worse then the first. He ignored the dog when it came up to visit him. He had ordered it away when he first came here, but now it came up the hill from time to time and went slinking around him with its tail tucked between its legs. It kept its face averted but rolled its eyes fearfully to look at him. Perhaps it remembered how sternly he had commanded it to go away from this sacred place so the spirits would not be disturbed by its presence. Perhaps it could hear spirit voices in the wind, or was frightened by the unnatural sound of his chanting. His tired voice became weaker. Sometimes he sounded like the croaking of a raven, then could only whisper with the dryness of his mouth and throat.

As soon as he awoke on the fourth day he went down to the creek to drink. Surely the hill was higher and steeper now. He stumbled and fell, then went down the slope, sliding and rolling. Finally he crawled on the gravel beside the flowing water. He drank deeply; than felt very ill and immediately vomited up all the water he had swallowed. After that he drank in small sips with long rests between. For a while he sprawled beside the stream like a warrior wounded in battle, but soon he began to feel much stronger. Three days without food do no harm to a strong young person and he was no longer thirsty. There was only a nagging guilt that he had yielded to his thirst and now the spirits might be displeased with him. But then he remembered that Little Owl had told him to drink on the fourth day and suddenly he no longer felt guilty. He was ready to resume his vigil. It took a long time for him to climb back up the slope.

# Chapter 20

## *The Shaman Loses Face*

The sun blazed and the wind howled through another long day. Finally he stared at the brilliant reds and yellows of a spectacular prairie sunset and watched as the mysterious sky people ignited their tiny twinkling fires. As the sky darkened a huge full moon rose up b behind his back, and finally the voice of the everlasting wind grew weak enough for him to hear the first coyotes singing their distant songs. In spite of his thirst and hunger his eyelids grew heavy and he dozed. Suddenly he awoke, startled and alarmed. Behind him among the rocks a voice was speaking. At first, ghost fear caused his heart to thump in his ears, but then fear changed to recognition. It was the voice of the Great Gray Bear! There were sniffs and grunts and an occasional growl mingling with a deep-toned, mumbling speech. After he turned to face the source of the sound the moon was shining into his eyes, blinding him to the thing that was lurking in the shadow cast by one of the looming rocks. As his eyes adjusted, he began to see that a part of the darkness was slowly moving, changing its position so that the ears on a huge head could be seen The ghostly bear was facing him, looking at him, seeing him clearly in the moonlight, no doubt seeing the fear on his face. He heard something like a muffled chuckle from the darkness followed by words that he could understand. "Do you not know me, Grandson? Ho, I will let you know who I am! Listen!" The bawling roar of a grizzly smote his ears. He reeled backward away from the dreadful sound, but righted himself quickly. Nearby, coyotes began to bark warningly.

Certainly this was not a dream. The totem bear was real! Its speaking voice continued. "Soon you will see the thing I have brought you as a gift. It is a thing you can wear around your neck so everyone will know who you are. They will know you are the warrior of the Great Bear. But this is not the reason I have come here. No, I came to bring a gift to your people. When I leave you will come forward and pick up the things I am leaving. You will place the symbol of the bear around your neck. Then you will hold the sacred bundle in both your hands. You will sit there praying until your elder brothel comes. When he comes you will greet him, calling him Monkon. From this day on you will always called him Monkon. You will promise to guard him and the sacred bundle. You will follow his commands always. And when you re return to the town of your father you will tell your fellow warriors what has happened here. You will tell them that they must always guard and obey the one called Monkon."

The spirit bear roared again. It roared the way it had roared on the day of the fight with the Pawnees. It roared in the way it had taught Gray Bear to roar. Now Gray Bear knew that he must respond. He tried to speak with the growling tones which his clan brothers use in their rituals, but his tired voice rasped and squeaked strangely. He said, "Oh, Great Gray Bear, Grandfather of all bears, I have heard your words. I will do these things that you have told me to do. As long as I live I will obey your commands." His voice was failing him but he went on trying to speak. Suddenly he was aware that the dog was there, pushing in front of him. It no longer had a fearful air. It began to growl fiercely and suddenly charged forward right at the dark place where the spirit bear was hidden. Gray Bear yelled at the dog to come back but it ignored him. He was horrified by the sacrilege—his dog: was attacking a sacred spirit thing! From the sound of its growls it seemed to have rushed on down the hill as if the Spirit Bear were fleeing from it. Gray Bear leaped to his feet and rushed after it. From down the slope he heard a bear roar, blending with the shrill cries of a dog in frenzied combat. Strangely the voice of his brother, Little Owl, seemed to be crying out down there as if a devil were attacking him. As Gray Bear peered down the slope he saw a strange sight in the moonlight. Little Owl was rolling on the ground entangled in an unfamiliar hairy robe. Yellow Face had seized the edge of the robe in his teeth and was tugging fiercely. The magician was kicking furiously at his attacker and trying to rise to his feet but the dog had the advantage because of the steep slope. Each time the shaman tried to rise he was thrown off balance again and dragged farther down the hill. At last he managed to free himself from the hairy skin and sprang away, leaving the dog to tussle with the lifeless object. Suddenly, Yellow Face seemed to realize there was no longer a living body inside the skin. He turned to slink away. Gray Bear had drawn back into the shadow of the rocks. He was gazing, open mouthed, at the scene before him. His thoughts had been tumbling in confusion but now they were becoming clear. Little Owl stood there in the moonlight, glaring at he dog furiously. Suddenly, with a series of violent motions he performed a remarkable feat. A short bow appeared in his hands and he dropped down into a peculiar crouching position with the bow held out in front of him, parallel to the ground. His two moccasined feet were holding the bow by pressing against its inside curve while his good left hand was pulling back the arrow and bowstring. And the arrow was pointing at the dog. Gray Bear grunted with surprise as he recognized in the curious posture, in the unusual position of the bow, the form of the mysterious being that had wounded him on that long-ago night in the Missouri woods. Now that "mysterious being" was going to shoot his dog! Gray Bear yelled, startling the shooter, spoiling his aim. The arrow struck a rock, then whirred away harmlessly down the slope. Now Gray Bear dashed forward and stood over his brother looking down at him. And Little Owl lay there on his back with the bright moonlight on his boyish face and, for once, his magician's composure was completely shattered.

His mouth actually twisted in a foolish grin. Gray Bear tried to look stern but soon felt his own face responding with a grin of triumph. Then he began to laugh. He laughed so hard he found it difficult to stand on the sloping ground. He sprawled on the ground and laughed some more He pointed at his brother and shouted a suggestion for a new name. "Man Who Sits-to-shoot." Little Owl countered weakly with "Dog Man." Gray Bear. Suggested "Fights with Dogs" and Little Owl Responded with "Man Easy to Fool." When they were tired of this sport, Little Owl showed Gray Bear the magnificent necklace of grizzly bear claws he had taken from the dead warrior. Gray Bear placed it around his neck and suddenly it seemed to him the great bear was there, holding him in its mighty grasp, protectively. He seemed to hear again its voice saying "everyone will know who you are. They will know you are the warrior of the great bear" And even though he knew these words had been spoken as a part of his brothers trickery they were planted in his mind forever And he saw that Little Owl was holding in his hands a leather pouch of mysterious design. He did not stare at it and no words were spoken, but he understood this was the sacred thing they had come so far to retrieve. He felt a strong protective feeling toward that bundle and toward his brother who was holding it. He suddenly felt impelled to speak and said: "We are finished here. We will go down this hill. I will drink and eat. Then we will sleep. Tomorrow we will go down the small river that leads to bigger rivers. All these rivers we have seen flow to the great one, Ne Sho D'say, the river that flows beside our home!

# Chapter 21

# *The Rivers flow Toward Home*

Under the morning sun Little Owl led Gray Bear to a brushy backwater of an unnamed river and showed him a hidden canoe that he had taken from the Elk River people. It was a crude affair of a wooden frame covered with buffalo hide and Gray Bear curled his lip in disgust as he looked at it, but Little Owl explained that by using paddles to keep this crude craft in the strongest current, they could go back to the place where these western rivers join the Smoky River in only a few days. From there, he said, it is not far to our fathers lodge.

They spent three quiet days going down the rivers. Gray Bear grumbled that they would become soft and weak sitting in this canoe which could not even be properly paddled, but he was secretly pleased and excited that they were on their way toward their homeland. He did not tell Little Owl, knowing he would disapprove, that it was his intention to leave the river soon and go on foot across the land directly to the town where Shining Light was waiting for him. He had no reason to believe she would be waiting, but sometimes a man really believes that which he wants to believe even though there is no reason for the belief. He was so intent on his own interests that he scarcely noticed that Little Owl had been seized by a mysterious sickness. The medicine man's face was hot with a fever and he seemed to have no interest in his surroundings. He had even stopped eating. Gray Bear gave little thought to the matter, thinking only that a medicine man should be able to cure his own illness. One evening they parted from each other in a manner that neither of them had planned. Little Owl, his voice rasping strangely, declared he would not leave the canoe to sleep on the ground. He said, "I want to drift on down the river tonight. I must carry the sacred bundle to our people. The spirits are very angry with me, they have not given me enough days. Ho, Listen! I fooled the spirits that guard the dead on their scaffolds. They thought I was a spirit as I climbed up there. I took the sacred bundle of our people and they were pleased. But then I took the bear claws that were part of the decorations the dead warrior would wear in spirit land and they were very angry. You must give that necklace of Bear Claws to me now. I will promise to return it to the spirits of that place. Perhaps then they will let me live."

Gray Bear was already out of their canoe, standing in the shallow water of the landing place he had selected. He stood there staring at Little Owl in disbelief. "I will not do this thing," he said, "and I say we are staying here in this grove of trees beside the river tonight."

Little owl tried to stand and come ashore. He wanted to face Gray Bear and persuade him that the necklace must be returned. But he was to weak and sick to stand in the canoe and as he fell back into the bottom of the craft the force of his fall shoved it out into the deeper water and it began to drift with the current. Gray Bear could have retrieved it. He started, as if to dash into the water, but his keen desire to go across the prairie to the big town and his reluctance to give up the necklace that was now his priceless symbol, held him motionless. For just a moment he felt regret that his brother was dying, and a superstitious urge to tear the bear claws from his neck and throw them into the river. But these feelings quickly passed.

He had stepped from the canoe with all his the weapons on his person, as any warrior would have done, and Yellow Face had leaped out to stand beside him. Their store of food was in the canoe but that was a small matter. He began at once to think of how he would find a trail to the south. Little Owl had vanished from his view and from his mind. When he left the woods which grew beside the river he was at the edge of a vast prairie which seemed to reach to the earth's edge. Soon he was running up a long prairie slope, breathing the South West Wind into his lungs, feeling the joy of being completely free

# Chapter 22

## *The Chase*

He was hunting in the woods just after dawn, carefully stalking a fat doe, when Yellow Face suddenly growled a warning, then dashed up the low ridge on their right, barking furiously. Before the dog reached the crest of the ridge, a large number of warriors appeared up there and came rushing down toward him.

He saw at once that they were Pawnees, and that they were too many to fight. He wheeled and dashed off on a course directly away from them. He felt no fear. He was a powerful runner, confident that he could stay ahead of anyone who chased him. He looked back to right and left to locate the ends of the line of warriors He altered his course slightly so that he was running out into the prairie, running toward the far off town at the center of the world. When he looked back again he saw that a few of the warriors directly behind him were gaining fast. He knew the strategy of a race like this. A few of their most confident runners would run as hard as they could to force him to do the same. They would drop out when they were exhausted and their slower companions would come on hoping to catch him when he was tiring. He increased his speed, running almost, but not quite, as fast as he could run. Regretfully, he threw away his war club and slipped the carrying strap of his quiver over his head, discarding it along with the now useless bow. In doing this he inadvertently slipped the bear claw necklace off over his head and dropped it. The nearest of his pursuers saw it lying on the ground and scooped it up, then struggled to place it around his own neck as he ran. Gray Bear knew that he could not maintain this furious pace much longer, but looking back he saw that the fastest of his pursuers had slackened their pace. Some of them were in bad shape, their legs failing with fatigue even as they made desperate efforts to run faster. They were falling back from their front runner, a slim fellow whose legs still seemed to have their power. He was still carrying a small, stone-headed club, which he now threw at Gray Bear. He seemed close enough for a good throw but he was very tired. The club came, spinning and bouncing past Gray Bear's feet. On a sudden impulse he snatched it up, stopped and wheeled to face his pursuer. The Pawnee was no coward. He drew his skinning knife and came right on, gasping a war cry with wheezing breath. Gray Bear had an instant of surprise as he saw the necklace of grizzly bear claws around the man's neck. But even in this instant he was swinging the club for a hard throw right at the man's head. It struck the brave but foolish runner right between his eyes. The man fell and Gray Bear wheeled and raced away with renewed confidence.

Gray Bear could run all day, especially if his life depended on it. The leading Pawnees had settled down to a steady pace that was little faster then the usual, travel dogtrot. They would follow his trail when they could no longer see him. He must find some way to shake of these troublesome pursuers. He was surprised when Yellow Face rejoined him. He had thought the Pawnees might have killed the dog. Gray Bear gasped out a greeting, "Ho, Big Wolf, I did not know you could run so fast. Now we will see how far you can run in one day." He changed his course to go behind a long prairie rise which would screen him from the Pawnees. He was running now among scattered herds of buffalo. He changed his course again so that he ran down a long shallow trough between two ridges. There was a large herd directly ahead and he noted that the west wind was on his back. Slowing his pace he trotted directly through the herd. The grazing beasts were scattered enough that he could do this, though he occasionally came close enough to cause a skittish cow to bolt from his path and several times big bulls turned to face and threaten him. He had a plan. On his belt he still carried a fire-making kit. As soon as he was through the big herd he dropped down on his knees in the dry prairie grass and began to work furiously with the small fire bow. Soon he had a spark which he blew into life and fed with a handful of dry grass. When he had a patch of burning grass, he worked with furious haste, lighting hand full of grass to form fast-burning torches which he used to spread the fire. Soon it was burning over a wide area in the gusting wind and the bison, ever wary of an age old enemy, prairie fire, began to run. They ran, as Gray Bear had known would, facing the wind. Soon the whole valley was roaring with the pounding of their hoofs. The Pawnees were in their path and while it seemed unlikely that experienced prairie-men would actually be harmed by a stampeding herd, the situation would certainly require their full attention for a while. As for Gray Bear, he was now running easily across the blackened ground, running to hide behind another prairie ridge which rose there to the east. He would soon turn, using his mysterious sense of direction and set his course directly toward the big town. Also he would begin to look for a place to rest. Up ahead he saw a low place with tall grass and a few weak trees. There might be water there and he was very thirsty.

# Chapter 23

## *The Wolf Clan*

Gray Bear was crouching beside a green and slimy slough, dipping the water with one cupped hand, drinking slowly as one must after a long run. The big dog was there beside him, panting, then drinking, then pausing to pant again. The great fire he had started was racing away with the wind. The billowing clouds of smoke were filling half the sky. The odor of burning grass was strong even where no smoke filled the air. The roar of the stampeding bison, running away from the fire, still came faintly to his ears but it was almost lost in the rumble of an approaching storm. He knew that the Pawnees who had been chasing him were at home in these vast prairies, they would find a way to avoid the bison and the fire was not actually moving toward them, but he had created a moving barrier between himself and his enemies. Now he had time to plan what he would do next.

Suddenly Yellow Face gave a warning growl. The dog was looking up at the top of the prairie rise just to the south of their location. Gray bear looked that way and saw a tall, slim person standing, staring down at him. The stranger held up his right hand, palm forward to show that he held no weapon. Gray bear did not respond, but he stood up and watched as more people came up from behind the ridge and stood there forming a line. He recognized them, they were Osages with their hair roaches in the manner of young men who have not yet earned their warriors feather. They were as many as the fingers on four hands. His thoughts jumped back to that morning in early summer when a party of warriors had followed him and tried to kill him. But of course they had been grown men, warriors all. He certainly was not afraid of a group of boys. He quieted the dog and stood, with an air of confidence and dignity, as the youngsters filed down the hill and approached him. He saw their chests were tattooed with the symbols of the wolf clan. The first young man in line greeted him again with the raised palm and began to talk. He said, "we know who you are. There has been much talk about you in the town. They say you counted two coups against that big warrior, Crazy Bear, in a fair fight. They say you travel with a spirit wolf that attacks armed warriors. They call you The Warrior of the Spirit Wolf. Is this the wolf here beside you?"

Gray Bear ignored the question and said, "Which of you is leader?"

The boy who had been talking bristled, he said, "Can you not see I am the leader?"

Gray Bear glowered at him and said, "I see no feather. Perhaps you are wearing a feather from that tiny bird that drinks from flowers?"

The other boys grinned broadly at this. The leader was not amused. He demanded, "What are you doing here in the land of the Osages?" Gray bear answered gruffly, "Can you not see that I am one of the people? The Panther chief, the one called Deer Stalker, wanted to adopt me as his son. Then men of the bear clan tried to kill me because of lies told by that old shaman, the bear shaman. I will return when he goes to the spirit land. Maybe I will come back sooner and send him to the spirit land."

The leader looked interested. He said, "That man has gone to the spirit land. People say another more powerful shaman used magic to get rid of him. We think it was the Panther Shaman who did it."

If Gray Bear was pleased by the news he did not show it. He asked, "Why are you young ones here? There are Pawnee warriors nearby. They will take your scalps and leave you lying here for the ravens to eat."

The leader answered, "We are from the hunting camp over there, two sleeps away, on the green river. The chief sent us to look for enemies. He said to us if you see Wichitas, shout your war cry and they will run away. But if you see Pawnees, run back and warn us. I stood and listened to what he said but I did not say I would obey him. I told my companions, I will not run. I will fight." He went back to his first question "Is this the spirit wolf that fights with armed warriors?"

Gray bear said, "This one is but a puppy beside the spirit wolf. But he is a warrior. He warns me when enemies are near. Men cannot see the spirit wolf, but those who have felt his teeth will talk about him as long as they live. But I am not here to answer questions. Ho, listen to me: I am warrior of the Grizzly Bear. I am warrior of the thunder gods. They came to help me when I was fighting Pawnees. I am warrior of the spirit wolf, he travels with me always. Now, I will go on with my fight against the Pawnees. I have sent fire to burn them. I have sent bison to trample them. The thunder spirits are coming now with their lances of fire to help me fight them. I will call the spirit wolf to run beside me and I will go to join them."

The boys were grinning again, amused by such heroic boasting. Gray Bear glowered at them as if he were a story teller trying to frighten children. He continued, "You Little Ones should run back to your mothers. But if there is one among you who wants to become a man, he can follow me." With that he turned and strode away to the west.

The boys stood for only a moment in stunned silence. Then they howled the war cry of the wolf clan and leaped forward to form a file back of Gray Bear. Soon they were singing a fierce war song as they followed him toward the roar of the approaching storm.

# Chapter 24

## *Chief Gray Bear*

The darkness at the eastern edge of earth was fading. The Morning Star still gleamed there, steady and bright, like a hole in the dark roof of sky through which light came from some unimaginable source. In the dark prairie around the Pawnee camp no creature stirred or called. The faint rustling of tall grasses in the dawn wind was accompanied by a sort of pulsing whisper as if the land itself were breathing. Perhaps the sound came from the sleeping bison that lay like dark mounds near and far. Perhaps it was the breathing of the Earth Mother herself, sleeping in the mysterious night like the Pawnee warriors who were lying there, under the willows beside a prairie slough. They had gone to sleep without fear, knowing they were in the land of their own people A single sentry was standing in their midst, staring at the star that was sacred to his people. His lips moved with the words of a prayer but no sound came from him. The prayer did not comfort him. He remained tense, aware of the uncanny stillness all around. The prairie is a living, breathing, thing with myriad ears and eyes and countless voices. Its silence now was like a shout of warning.

Not far away, a bird leaped from the grass and flew above the sentry's head. He knew its shape and its fast-beating wings. It was a meadowlark, a singer in the bright sunlight of spring and summer. Only some creeping terror in the dark place where it slept could have sent it flying before sunrise. The Pawnee opened his mouth to sound a warning. But his pride kept him silent. Some moons before, while on night duty, he had shouted an alarm and there had been no danger. His companions had taunted him mercilessly for his fearfulness. He thought it would be better to wait for another sign than to risk being taunted again. The sky grew brighter in the east. The sentry's heart slowed and his fear receded with the growing light. He almost smiled as he watched the few thin clouds, there where the sun would rise, turning from gray to yellow. Now it was safe to call, not in warning, but to awaken his companions. He opened his mouth to call, then grunted with the thud of an arrow in his chest. As he fell, tall figures rose up from the grass all about and charged into the camp.

Strangely the attackers did not yell. Their chief had asked them not to sound war cries until they were in the midst of their enemies. It had been his thought that they were twice out numbered here, and must be in among their enemies before arousing them. And it had been his thought that they should charge into the camp from every direction instead of with the sun at their backs, as was the age old custom. So their rush was strangely quiet; with only the soft thudding of their running feet on the matted grass until they were among the enemy warriors and their first blows fell. Then a howling yammer of wild cries seemed to fill the sky. It must have sounded to the Pawnees as if all the wolves in the world were howling at once. In the midst of the wolf cries the bawling roar of an enraged grizzly bear could be heard. Some Pawnees arose and fought and were overwhelmed. A few fled from the camp like rabbits running before a prairie fire. Soon Grandfather Sun had risen to witness the celebration of victory. The murderous war cries of the wolf clan changed to cries of exultation. The noisy celebration continued as the sun rose.

When it was over, Gray Bear assembled them into a group to hear what he had to say. They stood with gleaming eyes, listening respectfully, almost worshipfully. He said, "These were the runners who followed me when I was alone. They tried to capture me. "Ho, it was a great run that I gave them. Now, there to the north, where the Flat White River flows, there is another party painted for war. They are coming this way, I think. We will go to meet them. You are warriors now. You have proven your strength and your courage. There is not one coward among you."

Soon they were marching away to the north. Gray Bear sent out single scouts to the high places on the prairie, places where they could lie in the grass of a windy crest and look far away to north and west to see if enemies were coming. At the end of the day the westernmost watcher came running back. He was accompanied by two strangers. They were tall, gaunt men with their faces painted for war. They wore curious crowns of red-dyed feathers, big medallions of the shining white shells of the prairie rivers. One of them was wearing a necklace of grizzly bear claws.

Gray Bear recognized them at once as Kanzas, the western kinsmen of the Osage people. The man with the bear claws was a big talker and boaster. He declared the whole fighting power of the Kanza people, every man and boy able to carry a weapon, was marching north to punish the Pawnees. In the season just past, the Pawnees had stolen a young daughter of the preeminent chief of the Kanzas. Later, word had come that she had been killed, sacrificed to the morning star in that demon's ceremony for which the Pawnees were hated. The voice of the Kanza rose in rage as he told this. He smashed his warclub against the ground between his feet. Gray Bear stood there thinking of another chief's daughter and how this terrible thing could have happened to her. His voice shook with imagined grief and real rage when he said, "We will go with you. We will march with our brothers the Kanzas. We will show no mercy to those Pawnees." His young Osages leaped and waved their weapons and howled like wolves.

127

# Chapter 24

## *The Return*

It was a night of sickness and fear of death for the small shaman in the canoe. He drifted off to sleep from time to time, then awoke to stare up at the stars. Strangely there were no spirit voices in his mind. For once he longed for human companionship, for his mother and his father, even for his brother Gray Bear. Once he called to Gray Bear to help him paddle the canoe. But of course his brother was far away, somewhere up stream, no doubt sleeping in comfort in the woods with the awful necklace of bear claws around his neck, unaware that he was certain to die soon so the necklaces can be returned to its spirit owner. Little Owl's thoughts went back to the dead man rotting on the scaffold on that ghastly hill top where he never should have gone. He cried out in terror at this memory, "It was not I who went there. It was my spirit. My spirit took the sacred bundle, the bag containing the memories of my people. That was a good thing to do. But I —but it should not have taken the bear claws, the symbol that young man was to wear in spirit land. Those claws were not stolen from my people. They belonged to that young man alone, a symbol of his bravery. Now help me spirits to give that necklace back to him" But the spirits did not answer. There was only the gurgling of the river and the sounds of a few night creatures on the nearby shore. His voice was like a moan, "The spirits have deserted me."

Finally the night passed and dawn found the shaman still alive but still too ill to sit up in the canoe, much less to take up a paddle and guide it to shore near the village where he must deliver the sacred bundle. But suddenly he did sit up! He looked around in a dazed manner and said, "What Happened?"

For something had happened. Far away, up stream, and out on the prairie to the south, the Pawnee runner who had chased Gray Bear since dawn, pitched to the ground, his head cleaved by the axe thrown by the man he was pursuing. And, as he fell, some unseen entity must have snatched the Bear Claw Necklace from his neck for it was seen no more by human eyes.

When the morning sun was well above the tree tops, the people of the small village beside the Great Smoky River flocked to the shore to see a strange sight. A canoe of peculiar design, a contraption consisting of a wooden frame covered with buffalo skins, was being paddled ashore by a small man wearing a shaman's robe and with long hair blowing in the wind. That man brought joy to the people of the town: He had retrieved the sacred bundle, containing the memories of the people, from the western raiders who had stolen it. But he brought grief to his own family for he told them that the warrior son, the one called Gray Bear, had been killed earlier that day, probably by Pawnees.

Many moons would pass before this latter declaration was proven wrong by the visit of the distinguished War Chief, Gray Bear, and his beautiful wife, the one called Shining Light, to his native village on the Great Smoky River. By that time, the shaman had attained even more distinction among his people, amazing them with magic tricks and conjuring up terrifying images out of the darkness beyond their night fires. He was known to them only by the honored name of Monkon.